WOLF ON HORSEBACK

WOLF ON HORSEBACK

MERLE CONSTINER

SAGEBRUSH
Large Print Westerns

First published in Great Britain by ISIS Publishing Ltd.
First published in the United States by Ace Books

Published in Large Print 2011 by ISIS Publishing Ltd.,
7 Centremead, Osney Mead, Oxford OX2 0ES
United Kingdom
by arrangement with
Golden West Literary Agency

British Library Cataloguing in Publication Data
Constiner, Merle.
  Wolf on horseback.
  1. Western stories.
  2. Large type books.
  I. Title
  813.5'4–dc22

ISBN 978–0–7531–8750–0 (pb)

CHAPTER
ONE

Kyle Fentress sat easily in his saddle riding aimlessly cross-country. About mid-afternoon he hit the railroad and on impulse turned southward along it, following the berm of the tie-ends. He was twenty-two years old and slender, with the pinched impassive face of an old man. He had been born up north on the hardscrabble fringes of the Bear Paw Mountains, and really loved only two things, guns and cows. With exception of his saddle and gun belt, he rode as he was clothed, for all his saleable gear had long ago been converted into emergency food. The country around him was southeastern Wyoming, the year was 1889 and the season was late November. The last beef herd had been shipped and he was out of work, and like countless other cowboys, it was exist somehow until spring and the big May roundups.

Dusk went into night, and suddenly a short distance ahead, he saw rosy light beneath the tracks, silhouetting them in black. This, and the downward slope of the earth, told him that he was approaching a trestle.

The pocket beneath the trestle was a dry ravine, maybe fifteen feet from its floor to the tracks overhead. On a little ledge in the ravine's side a man sat by his campfire, its embers bright crimson against the blackness of the night. He wore denim work clothes as did Kyle, but whereas Kyle's were faded and patched, his had the stiff crinkly look of newness about them. His horse stood beside him. A big black with white stockings.

Beneath his hat brim was one of the meanest, stupidest faces Kyle had ever looked on. Flat, cunning-eyed, slimy-mouthed. On his knee was a tin plate crammed with food: three pork chops, four greasy fried eggs and a mound of beans wet with molasses. He glanced at Kyle, studied him for an instant, and resumed eating.

Kyle dismounted, and said, "Evening."

Without looking up, the man said, "Where do you work?"

It was insolently asked, but Kyle answered it.

"It's almost December," said Kyle. "I'm not working anywhere. I been following the chuck line."

It was a hard thing to admit when you came right down to it, but no cowman however respectable looked at it that way. When the off-season turned up and you were out of a job, you could either go into town and degrade yourself with a sorry job like saloon swamper or stable helper, or you could ride the chuck line.

Riding the chuck line you went from ranch to ranch, asking for work, hoping for work, but knowing there was no work, staying a few days, eating and sleeping, and moving on. It was all in the family really. Nobody thought wrong of it. Every cowboy did it sometime or other. You had to, to exist. Every rancher expected it; he'd done it himself when he was young.

"The Chuck Line Kid," said the man. "How you been making out?"

"Not good," said Kyle.

"Hungry?"

After a moment, Kyle said steadily, "Yes."

The man seemed not to hear him. Slowly he ate. After a moment he stretched out the plate in Kyle's direction and laid it on the ground. It contained three pork-chop bones, one half-eaten egg and a scattering of beans.

The man belched. "I've et all I can," he said. "I always like to leave a little for a hungry dog. Finish it."

Kyle stepped forward. He placed his boot under the rim of the plate and turned it over in the dust.

They stared at each other, the man grinning, Kyle impassive. Neither of them said anything.

Kyle swung into his saddle, rode out of the little pocket under the trestle, up the farther bank of the ravine, and once more onto the roadbed.

Down the tracks perhaps a half a mile a scattering of lights had come on, the lights of a small town.

He had seen that man before, once, fleetingly. It had been a year ago by a little stream in a clump of alder on the Montana-Wyoming border. It had been in the pre-dawn and Kyle had been saddling up after a night's camp, and the man had ridden up and taken a drink a short distance downstream. He had been riding all night and his horse was criminally lathered and choking on its own swollen tongue. The quick drink for the man, a quick drink for the horse, and then he was gone. Later, Kyle had heard him talked about. His name was Breathitt and he was a kill-crazy gunman from Idaho, running from the law.

It was Kyle's guess that this was the way he spent most of his life. Most likely that was what he was doing right now, up there under the trestle.

The town was called Gaynor, and he felt right away in his bones that it was a bad town — the kind he usually tried to stay out of. But a town, any town, meant food somewhere. He'd leave first thing in the morning. It didn't look like a bad town, a really dangerous town, but bad towns rarely did.

Main Street with its railroad tracks down the middle was wide enough on either side for five wagons abreast, and the double row of shops, houses and offices which faced each other across its expanse gave the impression in the night of a sort of elongated military station. Too, it seemed to be at least six blocks long, which made it fairly sizable. He came in hugging the north side of Main, near the wooden sidewalk. The lamp-lighted shops were decent enough, but the usual loafers in their doorways and by the hitching racks had more than the average sprinkling of hard-case characters. And he knew a hard case when he saw one, whether dressed in respectable gambler's black, or woolly, happy-go-lucky goatskin chaps.

There were about double the normal number of saloons, some of them pretty squalid; and no saloon stayed open unless it had the business. The thing that bothered him most was that at least two of the houses he passed had their blinds drawn and tacked to their inside sills. These certainly had to be parlor-houses, not residences. It had to be a mighty hell for leather town not to isolate its parlor-houses in some secluded section of their own.

He dismounted at a hitching rack, tied up Effie, his roan mare, and started down the boardwalk.

The problem now was to find some decent job, some little job, which would pay for a bite to eat and a place to sleep.

In town you were honor bound to pay with cash or work for anything you received. If you tried to ride the chuck line in town, that would be begging, asking for charity.

For the next half hour he went up and down Main Street, shop by shop, asking to do a little work, anything. Everywhere people shook their heads. Right now help was a glut.

Finally he entered a small shop with a sign which said, *Saddler & Harnessmaker*.

An old man in a little leather lap-apron was standing behind the counter talking to a girl. They seemed to be just socializing. The girl was tall, maybe an inch taller than Kyle, straight with black hair and blue-black eyes. She had a nice, friendly voice and Kyle just stood for a minute listening to her. Finally he cleared his throat and the old man asked what he could do for him. Kyle asked for work, any kind of work, to meet a pressing financial obligation. The man shook his head, earnestly and sympathetically.

5

The girl turned and faced him.

"What's your name?" she asked, and he told her.

"Where are you from?" she asked.

Her voice and her manner were almost as though she were a foreman in a bunkhouse gossiping with a new hand.

"Well, I'm from about everywhere," said Kyle, "as you probably guessed. My last job was at the BK ranch, up on Powder River. After we took 'em to the chutes and said goodbye to 'em, family and friends bid me goodbye too, until next spring."

"The BK?" said the girl. "How is Lucy?"

The BK was Bruce Kendall's spread. Lucy was his big male mastiff which had been misnamed as a pup by Kendall's daughter.

"Lucy's fine," said Kyle, quietly. "But you're trying to catch me, aren't you? To see if I'm lying to you. To see if I really know who Lucy is. If you'll excuse me, I'll get out of here. I ain't used to having my word doubted. I don't like this kind of talk."

"Wait a minute," she said, and he paused.

"Calm down." She studied him from boot-toes to hat-crown. "If you think I go around believing every cowboy that opens his mouth, you're still wet behind the ears. I just wanted to know a little more about you."

Slowly, slowly, he smiled.

"I'm Barbara Spencer," she said. "My father has a ranch just north of town. What kind of work are you looking for?"

"You mean they got a place for me?"

"No. At this time of the year, we're just like everybody else. I had something else in mind."

"What?"

"How long are you going to be in town?"

No longer than I can help, he thought; until daybreak, maybe. He said, poker faced, "That depends."

"All winter?"

"Who knows?"

Impressed, she said, "You must be a mighty good cow-hand. I never saw a good one yet that you could pin down, who would give you the time of day and swear to it. Well, let's go."

He followed her out of the shop. They started down the boardwalk.

"Could you be a handyman?" she asked.

"I guess. If I have to."

She explained. She had an uncle in town, a Mr. John Flake, who owned a small, well-stocked general store. For the past couple of years he'd had bad personal luck, one thing after another. His wife had died of heart trouble, and he himself was half invalided with asthma. His daughter, Melinda, about Barbara's age, did most of the running of the store but sometimes she too seemed to have a touch of her mother's ailment. Despite all this the store was prosperous.

"If it's prosperous, then why don't they have a handyman?" asked Kyle. "Why do they have to pick one up off the street, like me?"

"They have them, but they don't stay long. Most handymen are drifters."

"Could it be that Mr. Flake, with his asthma, works them half to death?"

"No," she said. "You'll see. My uncle is a fine, understanding man."

"I don't know what's wrong with me," said Kyle, "but if you say so, I believe it."

The store, called the Red Front, was on a corner; the corner of the building was cut off like the point of a wedge of cheese, and this was the entranceway. Kyle didn't open the door for Barbara, but he stepped back and let her go in first. This was more caution than courtesy.

He was startled by the inside but he was careful to look wooden.

The store, while not large, was like a big New York store. It had everything. Swinging on a chain overhead was a big camphene lamp. The floor planking was silver-cream from frequent scrubbings with lye, and the walls were a bright, glossy blue. There was just about everything you could imagine: gun-powder tea, and cutlery and cans of carriage varnish. There were ladies' hats, heavily flowered, and plush caps for men, blue and green and maroon. There were bolts of bright yardgoods, and a stack of Paisley shawls, neatly folded. There was a jar of rock candy. On the floor in front of the counter were bars of pig-lead. The mixture of smells, leather and kerosene and cinnamon, was wonderful.

A runty, sick-looking man came forward to meet them. His manner was mild and his voice was cordial. This was Mr. Flake. Barbara introduced Kyle to him, and they liked each other instantly. "And this is Miss Melinda Flake," said Barbara, "My favorite cousin."

Then Kyle saw the girl standing in the background, timidly in the shadows. She was a tiny blonde, almost emaciated, with a wan skin and delicate lavender in her deep eye sockets. She smiled hesitantly.

Barbara told who Kyle was and why he was here.

"You don't know how badly we need you," said Mr. Flake. "And while there will be carpentering and a few heavy things to move, the job isn't handyman at all. It's a little better than that, I hope. You'll be working generally with Melinda, and taking as much work as possible off of me."

"I'm just a cowhand," said Kyle, embarrassed.

"Give it a try," said Melinda encouragingly.

Kyle looked at the circle of expectant faces, and nodded.

"Well good-bye, Mr. Fentress," said Barbara. "I'll be seeing you again — I'm here for a visit every time I get in town."

When she had gone, Kyle stood and waited for further instructions.

"You're doing us a great favor, my boy," said Mr. Flake.

"Yes," said Melinda.

Kyle looked towards her, at her, and past her. The other one, Miss Barbara Spencer, had puzzled him. Sometimes he thought he liked her, sometimes he wasn't sure. This one was different. It came to him suddenly that he understood this one. She was quiet and shy. This one, he knew he liked.

Mr. Flake said, "The boy's been riding, Melinda. And no doubt's a little hungry. Fix up a bit of something in the kitchen. We'll be in shortly. I'm showing him his room."

Mr. Flake lifted a flap in the counter and they went through a door and down a passage at the rear. Melinda turned into the kitchen.

Kyle's room was at the end of the passage by the newel-post of the backstairs, near the alley door. To Kyle's eyes it was a very pleasant room, with an iron cot, a washstand and blue china bowl and pitcher, two chairs and an old carved-oak wardrobe. The small, cheerfully curtained window probably looked out on the alley, he decided. Here too the floor and walls were spick and span with frequent scrubbings. "How does it look?" asked Mr. Flake.

Kyle shook his head in appreciation and smiled.

They left the bedroom, went down the hall, and entered the kitchen. There was a plate served on the table and at Mr. Flake's gesture Kyle seated himself before it. The others sat down too. On the plate was a giant steak with a marrowbone. There was coffee too, and cold corn bread and butter.

"I picked a steak with a marrowbone," said Melinda timidly. "I thought you might like marrow."

"I do," said Kyle and began to eat.

He tried to eat slowly, as his mother in the dim past had taught him.

They watched him eat, Mr. Flake benevolent, Melinda beaming.

Suddenly, Kyle put down knife and fork. "I can't do it," he said.

"Why?" said Mr. Flake, bewildered.

"I'm hungry, but there's someone hungrier than me. Someone who never complains about it. That's my roan mare, hitched up the street."

"Finish your meal," said Mr. Flake softly. "I have the feeling you're the young man I've been dreaming about for some years now. This could be my lucky day and yours too. When you've eaten get your mare, take her to the Star Livery Stable and put it on my account."

Kyle gave him a deep, burning look, and Mr. Flake knew that he had made a friend.

A little later Kyle went uptown for Effie.

CHAPTER
TWO

When he returned from the livery stable to the Red Front Store, Melinda was alone in the shop, preparing to close for the night. Her manner toward him was neither friendly nor unfriendly, simply businesslike. She patted the folds out of the bolts of gingham and calico and restacked them. She closed the little iron petty-cash box under the counter and locked it with a key on a chain from her bosom. She double-bolted the front door. She then lowered the big camphene lamp on its ceiling rope, extinguished it and raised it in the dark on its counterbalance. Kyle watched her, wanting to help but not knowing what to do. When the lamp was out she said, "Father wants to see us upstairs."

Wordlessly, Kyle followed her behind the counter, into the passage and up a flight of steps into a short hall. They entered Mr. Flake's bedroom with its heavy red curtains and black walnut woodwork, arranged just as the late Mrs. Flake had left it. In the faint blossom of light from a candle on the table, Kyle took it in with interest. There was Mrs. Flake's conchological cabinet in a corner with a collection of dusty sea shells, pink and orange, looking to Kyle like fleshy open mouths.

Mr. Flake, with a shawl about his shoulders, sat limply on the edge of the bed. Now he looked really sick. "What's wrong, children?" he asked. "Is something the matter?"

"I thought you wanted to see me," said Kyle.

"Papa," said Melinda tensely. "Mr. Fentress has been trying to molest me!"

The silence which followed was electric.

Mr. Flake closed his eyes wearily, and opened them. He said, "Kyle, I liked you on sight.'

Softly, Kyle said, "Thank you, sir."

Mr. Flake put a sarsaparilla cough-candy into his mouth.

After a moment he asked mildly, "Have you been molesting Melinda?"

"I don't even know what molesting means," said Kyle. "But I sure think I know from the way everybody's acting." He flattened his lips. "No, I didn't."

Mr. Flake turned to his daughter. "And what do you say to that?"

"He means not intentionally," said Melinda. "Well, that's a relief. I accept his apology."

Gently, Mr. Flake said, "You're really a decent boy, aren't you? You see, here you are in my house and I really have to know."

"No," said Kyle, "I'm not decent. Law officers, across three states say I'm a disgrace to eternity." He stood stiff and pale. There was ice and iron in his voice. "But when I give you my word it's good. That's the only thing I really own, my word. And I sure ain't going to abuse it."

"It's good enough for me," said Mr. Flake. "We have these little troubles now and then, not exactly like this one, but troubles. Let's all forget it and go to bed."

The big wooden clock in the corner clicked and clucked, like a mother hen talking softly to her brood of springs and cogs and wheels.

"Goodnight, Papa," said Melinda.

Kyle and Melinda left the room.

Out in the hall with the bedroom door closed behind them she said, "Don't touch me."

"Ha," he said.

They stood for a moment, considering each other.

"Why did you say that terrible thing to your father?" he asked.

"Because."

"Because why? What you got agin me? You never saw me before tonight."

When she didn't answer, he said, "What do you want?"

"I want you to pack up and leave," she said.

He could hardly believe his ears. Earlier, before her father and Miss Barbara, she had acted so friendly. "Why?"

"We don't need anyone coming here, breaking into our lives, ruining everything. We're very happy here and we don't need any outsiders. First it was my mother and my father and me. Then my mother died. And my father and I don't have anything but each other. And that's all we want. We don't want strangers coming between us."

Thoughtfully, he rubbed the side of his jaw.

14

"This could be just the beginning," she said. "You'd better leave tomorrow."

"No," he said calmly. "If you'd said I was trash, and a gun-throwing tramp, which I am, then I'd have left before you could have closed your mouth. Or if you'd made fun of my table manners, or my schoolin', which aren't much better than zero. Or if you'd just politely asked me to go. But they's somethin' in my elements which bucks up when people try to *force* me to do somethin'."

After a pause she said, "You're really not scared of me, are you?"

"Not too scared," he said. "Let's put it that way."

She appraised him carefully.

"What are you really scared of?"

He pondered for a moment. "Well, I'm scared of a bad cartridge that might blow out the breech of your rifle in your face. And I'm scared of diphtheria. Though I've never seen any. Just heard about it."

Down in his bedroom, he put his gun and gun belt in the compartment at the bottom of the washstand. He was going to stay here as long as Mr. Flake wanted him. Until spring roundup, if things worked out that way.

Next morning Kyle had himself braced for anything, but nothing happened. Melinda was sweet as honey. And even friendly. But he had seen her friendly before, and knew how quick and terribly she could change. Mr. Flake, when Kyle had any business with him, seemed just like before, cordial and a little sick, but there was something in his manner, some shadow in his eyes, which told Kyle he knew exactly what Kyle had been through, and that he deeply appreciated the fact that Kyle hadn't vanished during the night.

The first three days went smoothly. Kyle's work seemed to be a mixture of little things. He unpacked boxes and barrels, put merchandise on the shelves, and sometimes, very occasionally, he even waited on a customer. At the beginning he thought these trivial contributions to the shop were nothing, that he wasn't really needed, then gradually he realized that he was doing exactly what he had been hired for, to take the pressure off of Mr. Flake. He did it carefully and conscientiously, as he did any job assigned to him, but he never got to like it. He got a couple of hours off every day in late afternoon, when business was slow, and an hour off after supper; which was more than Melinda and Mr. Flake took.

At least once a day he visited Effie at the livery stable.

He wanted them to know him there. There was a belief among cowboys that certain town livery stables cheated in their feeding of horses, because a horse couldn't report to its master, so the thing to do was to show a big interest in your mount, let the stable know by your manner you wanted the best of treatment.

It was on his fourth day with Mr. Flake that the strange thing happened.

That night he went to visit Effie after supper.

As stables went, the Star was a big one. It was on the other side of Main Street, across the tracks, and if you included the corral beside it, it spread out almost a half a block. The building itself was huge, of unpainted lumber, gray and weathered and delapidated. Its whole front was open, its big double doors pulled back, and a small side road turned in here directly from the street. Inside, it was a big, dim cave, smelling of horse dung and urine and whiskey and cigar butts. The office was just within the door on the righthand side, and the stalls, horses' rumps facing inward, mangers facing outward, were down the long timbered cavern at the rear. Effie was about halfway down, to the left. The place seemed empty.

She had a kind of soft, lippy whistle, like nothing else in this world, which she sometimes gave to show her affection for Kyle. And she gave it now as he stepped into the stall to see if she was well-groomed.

He was running his hand over her back, talking to her, when he happened to glance out at the concourse of the stable behind him.

A stall door across the way opened and a man came out leading a big black horse, saddled. It didn't have white stockings now, but it sure as heck was Breathitt's horse, the horse Kyle had seen a few evenings ago under the trestle. Around the horse's shanks where it should have been white, it was glossy black. Like hair-dye.

The man wasn't Breathitt, either. He was a complete stranger to Kyle, a lithe, catlike man, bleak-faced, dressed like a shabby stockman but wearing two guns. One was on his thigh, in sight, and one was under his arm, bulging his canvas jacket.

He mounted the black and rode it leisurely out of the rear of the stable.

The hand that held the reins was smeared black. The horse had just been dyed.

A blowsy-looking stable helper came ambling by.

Kyle said, "Who owns the big black?"

"The horse with the white stockings? I didn't catch the feller's name. Big, with a meaty kind of face, wearing new work clothes."

"When did he bring his horse in?"

"Last night about midnight."

"Who was it that just took her out?"

"Is she gone? I didn't see her go. This is supper time and the stable back here is generally empty at supper time. Seems like we're always shorthanded. The same man must have took her out that brought her in. Nobody would horse-steal from a livery stable. It's too dangerous. Why you so interested?"

"I just like horses."

"So do I," said the helper. "The kickin', bitin', stompin', mean-tempered rascals."

Back at the Red Front, Kyle was in the storeroom wondering just what had happened at the stable, and unpacking a box of ribbon spools and thinking, How did I ever come to this, messing around with ribbons? when Barbara Spencer came into the passage from the alley. He gave her a good hard look. He hadn't seen her since the night she'd got him this job. Right now, her eyes seemed a little red.

He walked out into the hall. "I got a crow to pick with you," he said under his breath. "You know what you got me into here?"

"You mean Melinda?" she said, also softly. "Has she been trying to get rid of you?"

"She tried it once. And then gave up."

"Maybe she's getting to like you."

He didn't bother to answer. He just glared.

"This is not time to quibble," she said gravely. "I'm bringing bad news. And I'd appreciate it if you'd come along and listen to it."

They gathered in the kitchen, Melinda and Mr. Flake, Barbara and Kyle, and sat around the table. If a customer came in out front, Kyle knew, the bell over the door would cut loose like a steamboat bell. Melinda made coffee but no one seemed to want any.

"Father's been shot through the shoulder," said Barbara. "He's not dead, and he's not going to die, or so the doctor says, but he's in a mighty bad way."

"Who shot him?" said Kyle.

"How did it happen?" demanded Mr. Flake.

"It happened yesterday morning," said Barbara. "Out on our north range. This man came riding up to him and shot him and left him on the ground for dead. He lay there all day yesterday, all last night and all day today. We thought he was riding line. This afternoon a neighbor found him and brought him home."

"Who did he say shot him?" asked Kyle.

"A stranger," said Barbara. "A man on a big black horse with white shanks."

Kyle described the man in the stable. "Slimish, easy-moving, wearing two guns, one under his white canvas jacket?"

This startled them. Gently, Mr. Flake said, "It couldn't be. The man you mention sounds like Charlie Minnifee, a small rancher but a pillar of the county."

"And highly respectable," said Melinda.

"Where did you see Mr. Minnifee?" asked Barbara curiously.

They all seemed mighty interested in Mr. Minnifee.

"How do I know where I saw him?" said Kyle. "I been in town four days, I could have seen him any place. Maybe it was in the livery stable. Someplace."

"The man that shot my father," said Barbara, "was a big hulking man with a toad-face, and wearing brand-new denim work clothes."

Kyle thought it over. Killing was said to be Breathitt's livelihood. He had been brought in to kill someone, and that someone had to be Mr. Spencer. But he had been too sure of himself, and hadn't quite pulled it off. Who brought him in, whose money had he taken for the job? That man had to be Mr. Charlie Minnifee.

While they watched his impassive face, Kyle reasoned it out coldly. The horse, the stable, and what happened there. Say, after the shooting Breathitt had brought his black into town, stabled it, and spent the night at a hotel. Come morning he'd begun to worry about those easily-identifiable white stockings and hadn't called for it. Hadn't called for it, but had had his employer, Minnifee, fetch it. That made sense, good sense. It was the very thing a man like Breathitt, who lived in constant watchfulness, might do.

20

Ten to one, Breathitt was hiding out at Minnifee's spread right now.

What in the hell was going on here?

He had seen this pattern before, in three other states, and it always pointed up to some kind of mighty bad trouble. If something wasn't brewing, why didn't Minnifee, so respectable and all and with more than enough guns, take care of Mr. Spencer personally?

Kyle said, "Your father and this Mr. Minnifee, are they friends or enemies?"

"Neither," said Barbara. "They're just two hard-working cattlemen who happen to live in the same county. Actually, they scarcely know each other."

After a pause Kyle said, "The man who shot your father, Miss Spencer, is named Breathitt."

They looked at him. He spoke with such authority, with such quiet certainty, that no one doubted him. Suddenly he was in a world of his own, and everyone sensed it.

"Breathitt hires out in range wars, usually," said Kyle. "Don't tell me there's a range war around here that I don't know about?"

"Definitely not," said Mr. Flake.

"Is there one makin' up?"

"No to that also," said Mr. Flake. "Or we'd know it; the whole county would know it. There's nothing secret about a range war. Nothing. They take a long time building. And finally some little thing happens, some trivial little incident."

"Like Mr. Spencer getting shot off his horse."

Nervously, Barbara said, "I'm spending the night here. Will you ride out to our place with me tomorrow and talk with father?"

"If Miss Melinda can spare me," said Kyle.

"I can spare you," said Melinda.

CHAPTER
THREE

They left Gaynor after an early breakfast and headed
east, moving leisurely, for Barbara had explained to
Kyle that her father's ranch, the S-Diamond, was only
half a day's ride. At first Kyle rode to one side, lagging
a little, not to impose his presence upon the girl, but
Barbara soon corrected that by drawing him into
conversation. Before long they were riding stirrup to
stirrup. He had brought along his gun belt because out
in the bunch grass he felt crippled without it.

The grass was poor just out of Gaynor, but after a
while it became lush, and Barbara announced, "We're
on S-Diamond land."

Everywhere there were cattle, and he was interested
to see that they were all young ones, yearlings.

They all seemed to be fine specimens too, no lame
ones, big jaws, or runts. He said, "These Texas
critters?"

"Arizona," she said. "They came in last summer.
They're just beginning their double-wintering."

This was a new thing, just happening. And being an
old-style cowman, he wasn't quite sure he approved.
Northern ranchers were shopping in the deep south,
buying yearlings, bringing them north and grazing

them until they matured. On northern grass they would gain as much as two-hundred pounds over what they would put on back where they were born. And a Wyoming stockman could pick them up down there as cheap as fourteen dollars a head, maybe cheaper.

"A southern yearling or two-year-old," said Kyle, "eats like he is starved, like he's crazy."

"Usually, he is starved," said Barbara. "The ranges back where they come from have often been overstocked. They've passed the saturation point."

"But here in Wyoming we've grass enough to feed all of Texas and New Mexico, and always will have. Isn't that right?"

The new vogue had brought with it a terrible scare, and this was it. Kyle had heard it around a hundred campfires. It was exactly like the sheep scare had been in the old days down in Pleasant Valley. Ranches with bank accounts brought in yearlings (little ranches could make the grade in cash), and Wyoming grass would go down to its roots, the roots would die, and the plains would become little better than deserts. It was killing the goose that laid the golden egg. He said so to her.

Angrily, Barbara answered, "Where did you first hear that? In somebody's barbershop?"

He'd first heard it in a poolroom in Deadwood, but saw no need to say so.

She said, "You should be working for Mr. Charles Minnifee."

Well, he thought, here comes Mr. Minnifee again.

"He says that?" asked Kyle.

24

"To everybody. All the time. He's got a mania on the subject."

Kyle changed the subject. "Your father knows how to pick good yearlings."

"He doesn't pick them. He doesn't even own them. He doesn't do much ranching anymore, he's getting a little old. These belong to our neighbor, the LLL Ranch. He just rents grazing rights."

So he was right on top of that big cow-factory, the LLL and hadn't even realized it. Lowden, Lokely, and Lamont — the mammoth eastern company with its headquarters in Boston, and with a touch of the Bank of England in its veins. There wasn't a cowboy on the plains who wouldn't grudgingly admit they were topnotch stockmen. This ranch, their eastern Wyoming branch, was known as the Lochinvar.

"Lowden, Lokely, and Lamont," said Kyle. "I can't seem to make up my mind whether I like them or hate them."

"Like them, then," said Barbara. "I do."

The S-Diamond house, when they came up to it, pleased Kyle, but he made no comment. It was set in a sparse grove of cottonwoods, near a sweet-water stream. The house itself was a square, white box, low-eaved, with sheds and outbuildings, a blacksmith shop, cribs, and a barn flanking it at its side, forming an open U with it. There was no nonsense about it, no pretention. It had the feel of comfort and tranquillity. A saddled, cinnamon-colored horse was tied to a post before the front door.

"We seem to have company," said Barbara as they approached.

"Who?" asked Kyle.

"I'm not sure," said Barbara. "I think I know but I can't be right."

Kyle dismounted, tied Effie beside the cinnamon and followed Barbara to the barn. When she had dismounted he unsaddled her horse and turned it into a stall.

Crossing the ranch yard to the house they entered the front door. A worried-looking little gray-haired woman, Barbara's mother, met them distractedly in the parlor, welcomed Kyle pleasantly and firmly enough under the circumstances, and pointed to a curtained doorway to her left. "Mr. Minnifee is in there with him," she said. Under her breath she added, "I don't know why."

Kyle followed Barbara across the parlor. She pulled the curtain to one side and they stepped into a bedroom.

The walls were papered with pink roses on silver trellises, a little water stained here and there, and the bare pine floor was gay with brightly-colored scatter rugs. Against one wall, taking up about a quarter of the room, was a four-poster bed, and on it was an elderly man with a salt and pepper goatee. He was half sitting, propped up by starched pillows, and a bandage showed at the neck of his nightgown. He was talking. His voice was placid, but his face was tight with pain.

Facing him from an easy chair by the window sat Minnifee, the graceful, bleak-faced man Kyle had seen at the Star Stables. He was still wearing the gun at his thigh, plus the gun under his white canvas jacket, in his armpit.

There were introductions all around and Kyle put on his sleepy, no-brains-at-all look.

Mr. Spencer said, "I appreciate your interest, Mr. Minnifee, but I never saw him before. He just rode up and shot me off my horse and rode away. Why, I haven't the slightest idea. I think he was a stranger to the community and that by now he's long gone."

Minnifee said, "I'd like to talk to some of the other gentlemen-ranchers hereabouts, and form a little party to run him down. For you."

"Not for me," said Mr. Spencer. "Those things are for the law."

Kyle said blandly, "All them fellows told me wrong."

Minnifee turned to him. "What fellows? Told you wrong about what?"

"All them fellows around Gaynor," said Kyle. "The ones loafing around the feed store, them sitting on those benches on the depot platform, them at the Acme Saloon, all of them. They said you hated Mr. Spencer. That you been preaching around that this yearling grazing is an abomination to the range."

Minnifee's black eyes became flat, and a light like a little golden worm glowed in their centers. Here was a man, Kyle knew, who went instantly savage.

When he spoke, however, his tone was careless and arrogant. "Any disagreement I might have with S-Diamond on the subject of ranching is an opinion only, and actually with LLL."

When everyone remained silent, Minnifee said, "I may think Mr. Spencer's sympathies are wrong. But that's his business."

"These talking fellows," said Kyle. "They say you hold it against Mr. Spencer especially, because he rents his grazing to LLL. They say you claim he used to be a rancher like anybody else, and now he's gone over to the other side. And you figure that makes him the worst."

Barbara stared at Kyle as he spoke. As he stood there, spinning off what they both knew were fabrications, with a poker face.

"You seem to be pretty much of a talking fellow yourself," said Minnifee. His mouth was a little slit of teeth.

"Did I say something wrong, Mr. Spencer?" said Kyle.

Mr. Spencer, who had seen some pretty strange cowhands in his day, wearily shook his head.

"Just who are you, anyway?" said Minnifee frigidly.

"Just a cowhand out of work," said Kyle. Suddenly, as though it were an inspiration, he said, "You couldn't use me out at your place, could you?"

Minnifee ignored him.

Angrily, stiffly, he got to his feet. He swept his glance to Barbara and her father, nodding good-bye, and left the room.

A minute later they heard him outside the open window, mounting and cursing his horse.

To Kyle Barbara said, "But you've got a job. Papa, he's working at the Red Front."

"That was just a joke," said Kyle. "He seemed to care so little for me, I wanted to see if he'd bust out in flames."

On his bed, Mr. Spencer grinned.

Kyle stayed for noonday dinner. A little sewing table was brought in for him, and he ate in the bedroom with the wounded man. Twice Barbara tried to turn the conversation to Breathitt, but each time a warning glance from Kyle brought her to silence. They talked mainly about the BK up on Powder River, Kyle's last job. The Spencers had once known Bruce Kendall and his family intimately, and there were dozens of questions to be answered.

Finally, when Kyle had finished his meal and murmured his thanks, Mr. Spencer said, "I take it this is just a social visit from you, Mr. Fentress?"

He was a shrewd old man and knew there must be purpose behind his trip out here.

"Well, it's turned out to be a social visit," said Kyle. "And a mighty nice one. But I really came because Mr. Flake ordered me to."

"Ordered you to?" said Mr. Spencer, surprised. "Why?"

"He was worried about Miss Barbara making the trip alone with all this shooting going on."

"So was I," said Mr. Spencer. "And thank you."

He arose, wished Mr. Spencer good health and left the room with Barbara following him.

Outside the house she stood by his stirrup as he swung into his saddle.

"How far is it to the LLL?" he asked. "And how do I get there?"

"It's about six miles due east," she said. "What business have you got there?"

"Mustn't ask personal questions," he said, and smiled.

Despite herself, she smiled back.

"One thing more," he said. "Who is the boss?"

"The manager? Mr. Lucas Grinnell."

Due east he rode, the sun hot overhead, the air about him a sultry, powdery copper. This was a country of sweet-water streams, not alkali, and grassy bowls, now yellowed by the coming winter. Everywhere were peaceful looking cattle. He rode slowly, enjoying himself, enjoying the nearness of the cows. About two o'clock he came over a rise and descended a slope, and two horsemen came out of a clump of scrub at a lazy lope. They rode up to him, danced their horses to a casual stop, and somehow, in the process, blocked his way.

They were both competent looking hands, and a little too heavily armed for normal times. One was elderly, sun-blackened and calm; the other was young, with a flattened nose. The young one bristled with hostility.

They weren't gunmen. Kyle had the feeling they were crack cowhands, just doing their duty as they were told to do it.

"You know something?" Kyle said pleasantly. "I bet I'm an inch over on Three L land."

When they made no answer, he said, "I'm from Mr. Spencer. I got a message for Mr. Grinnell."

They relaxed. The older one pointed. "Straight ahead. Over the hill."

The younger one said solicitously, "How's Mr. Spencer making it?"

"I ain't no docter," said Kyle, "but I should say he's been mighty hurt."

They parted their horses and he rode through them.

There was no doubt about it. The Lochinvar was in a state of alarm. Or at least of alert. A little gunpowder touched off by a man like Breathitt, at the wrong time, the wrong place, could start a tornado. An outfit like the LLL, though, would think at least twice before it would take up arms. Maybe the excitement would die down, and it would all blow over.

The Lochinvar headquarters, when he came to it, turned out not to be just a ranch house, but a little settlement in itself. Counting everything, it had about twelve buildings laid out in an X, like a village crossroads.

To the left as he rode in was a long, low building which had a sign on it saying, OFFICE. Down its front ran a slab-roofed porch which gave a thin, gray shade, and was no protection at all from the searing sun. Kyle wiped the sweat from his throat. It was these freakish days in the autumn, these short, sultry nightmare returns to summer, which were so bad on man and cattle. In two days there could be blizzards, ice crust, and howling winds.

Kyle dismounted, tied Effie to a rail and entered the office.

He found himself in a small room, whitewashed. It was frugal and austere, with a big battered mahogany desk that looked as though it had been barrel-rolled all the way from Boston. Behind the desk sat a man in crinkled, dusty-black broadcloth. He was a youngish man, with round fish eyes and a jaw like a block of grindstone. He was an easterner, all right, but he was anything but soft. When Kyle came in, he sat back in his chair and took a funny-looking wad of cigars from a drawer. That's what they were really, a wad, all twisted together. He untwisted one, put it in his mouth and lit it. It was shaped like a corkscrew. He didn't offer one to Kyle.

"Mr. Grinnell?" said Kyle.

The man studied Kyle indolently, and nodded.

He was just too casual about it.

He himself was feeling the alarm and fever that was going through the ranch over Mr. Spencer's attack and didn't care much to see a hard-case stranger standing before him, unannounced. He was making every effort to show he wasn't even interested.

This, Kyle decided, was a man who was really on edge.

Kyle told him who he was, that he worked for Mr. Flake, and that he had just come from Mr. Spencer's. He didn't mention Minnifee in any way.

"All right," said Grinnell. "What do you want?"

What Kyle had wanted was two things, and each of them had been pretty much accomplished to his satisfaction. First, he wanted to get the feel of the ranch and see how it was responding to the shooting. It hadn't reached the danger point. Yet. But it was sure buzzing. Second, he wanted a look at Mr. Grinnell, to form an opinion as to just what kind of a man he was. He was fairly well satisfied on this point, too. If you got behind that pale Boston skin, Kyle decided, you'd find Mr. Grinnell all panther.

He wasn't mixed up in this, he kept telling himself, but he wanted to know these things because of Barbara. He wanted to know if things continued, and pressure got even worse against the S-Diamond, say with barn burnings, would Grinnell get into action and throw his strength behind the Spencer family?

He sure would, Kyle decided. He was already counting himself in. He was as nervous as a cat, expecting trouble.

"You're not going to believe this," said Kyle. "But I don't want nothing at all. I come all the way out here just to look at you and your spread. You're famous, and the Lochinvar's famous, and I didn't want to pass them by while I was in the neighborhood."

"I don't find that hard to believe," said Grinnell: "Have a cigar?"

"No, thank you," said Kyle. "I'd better be getting back."

Kyle went outside. He was standing on the narrow porch thinking things over when a wispy-looking cowboy came up to him and asked, lowering his voice, "You riding the chuck line? You hungry? Come with me to the cookhouse. We'll fix you up."

He was all mouth, with a big happy grin and Kyle figured the grin was permanent. He liked him on sight.

"I'm Kyle Fentress," he said. "How are you knowed?"

"They call me Green River," said the wispy cowboy. "Pleased to meet you, Mr. Fentress."

"To answer your kind question," said Kyle. "I was riding the chuck line a short time back, but I've turned respectable. I'm working in a store."

"In a store?" said Green River, in horror. "'Minds me one winter, with no work and starvin's, and one thing and another, in Phoenix. I worked in an umbrella shop, mending busted parasols for ladies."

"I didn't hear you," said Kyle. "And don't never tell nobody else."

It was early candlelight when he got back to Gaynor and the Red Front.

It was about three o'clock in the morning, and he was in his bedroom sleeping like a log, when there was a hammering at his door. He put the bed sheet around his shoulders, and answered it.

It was Melinda in a dressing robe. She said quietly, "A rider has just come and gone, from the S-Diamond. My uncle is dead."

"Mr. Spencer?" said Kyle. "I'm sorry."

This was a new Melinda. There was no fantasy here.

"Someone came up to the window in the night," she said, "And shot him as he lay on his bed. This time it worked."

Suddenly he knew he was in the family now. That she trusted him, and he could trust her. The revelation almost unnerved him.

Finally, he said, "That was what Minnifee was doing there this morning, pretending to visit him. He was finding out just where your uncle's bed was, and how he could be killed in the night, from the outside."

"Did Mr. Minnifee kill my uncle?"

"Had it done," said Kyle. "But it's all the same. The actual killing, likely, was done by Breathitt."

"What shall we do?"

"You don't do anything," said Kyle. "Except forget what I just told you."

CHAPTER
FOUR

It wasn't until noon next day that he was able to get away from the Red Front. He made directly for the courthouse, to talk to the sheriff. He wanted to find out what the official position on Mr. Spencer's shooting was. He wouldn't know just how much talking he should do himself until after he had had a look at the local sheriff.

There were as many kinds of sheriffs as there were humans, and a town like Gaynor might cough up a pretty scummy one. Besides, it was Kyle's lifelong code not to mess with the law until the law messed with him.

The courthouse was not large, but it was impressive-looking. It was of brick, two stories tall, with the lower floor half-sunk below ground level, surrounded by a sunken areaway topped by a rusty, iron-pipe railing. At the bottom of the areaway were old cigar butts, horsesale announcements, dead leaves, and other accumulated rubbish. Kyle climbed broad steps to the front door, entered, and found himself in a wide, empty corridor smelling of kerosene and whiskey. To his left, wooden stairs descended in half-light and a gold hand pointed to lettering on the wall that said,

36

Sheriff's Office. He went down the stairs, found the door he was after, and stepped inside.

There were dodger posters tacked to the dirty-white plaster walls, and a calendar from a seedhouse showing a golden cornucopia spilling out such big garden vegetables that they were scary. A man sat behind a desk, a knotty, middle-aged man with a sad, drooping mouth and baby-blue eyes. He had shaved that morning all right, but in a rush, and his face was mottled with patches of brassy stubble that the razor had missed. Wearily, he was rubbing the back of his withered neck with liniment. He seemed a man of troubles and ailments, trials and tribulations. "I don't know who you're looking for, son," he said. "But I'm Sheriff Jepson."

"You're the man," said Kyle. "How are things out at the S-Diamond?"

"Mrs. Spencer and Barbara are taking it brave," said the sheriff. "They're pretty fine people."

"Yes," said Kyle.

"I'll tell them you inquired," said the sheriff. "But I didn't quite catch your name."

"Kyle Fentress. I work at the Red Front. Have you got the man yet?"

"No," said the sheriff apologetically. "And maybe we never will. But I'll do my best."

Kyle gave him a quick look and glanced away. Most sheriffs would have said, "We're working on an important lead, and expect results soon," or at least would have looked mysteriously satisfied, but Sheriff Jepson looked miserable.

This, Kyle decided, might or might not be an incompetent sheriff, but Kyle was certain he was honest, conscientious and hard working.

An eerie sensation came over Kyle. He had a feeling that when Sheriff Jepson said, "I'll do my best," that was exactly what he meant.

"Sheriff Jepson," said Kyle. "Listen to this." Painstakingly, he told him his story about Minnifee and the scene in the livery barn, about the black horse with the white stockings made black. He told him about Breathitt, and Breathitt's background. He implied, and labored the point so that the sheriff wouldn't miss it, that it was Breathitt, hired by Minnifee, who killed Mr. Spencer.

The sheriff listened politely, but skeptically.

Kyle asked, "When you were out at the Spencers' this morning, did you find any sign?"

"We found sign, but it was pretty useless," said Sheriff Jepson. "A horse had been there, nearby, but his hooves had been wrapped in rags or burlap. It might have been any horse."

When Kyle looked angry, Sheriff Jepson said, "I have to serve a paper out by Mr. Minnifee's ranch this afternoon. I might as well drop in and look around. But I won't find nothing. Mr. Minnifee isn't that kind of a man at all. He's a respectable citizen."

Kyle nodded curtly and started for the door.

Sheriff Jepson put the liniment bottle on the desk-top and said, "I don't suppose you ever need liniment, you're too young and healthy. But if you ever do, try some of this. I make it myself. It's so pure you

38

could almost drink it. All you need is alcohol, cayenne pepper, and turpentine. You say you're riding out the chuck line at Mr. Flake's?"

"I said I was working there."

"Where did you work before you came to Gaynor, if you don't mind answerin?"

"I do mind answerin', but I will. My last job was at the BK ranch, up on Powder River. It's run by Mr. Bruce Kendall. You know it?"

"Simmer down. Yes, I know it."

"They got a male mastiff named Lucy."

"Is that a fact? I hadn't heered. Who lives south of Mr. Kendall?"

"I could tell you, but I ain't going to."

"A widow woman named Thorpe lives south of the Kendalls. And who lives due west of *her*?"

"Take me or leave me," said Kyle, "But don't prod me around."

Suddenly, wonderfully, the sheriff was grinning.

Back at the Red Front, in the kitchen, Kyle found Melinda and Mr. Flake with black voile and artificial flowers from the millinery counter, making a funeral wreathe for the front door of the Spencer ranch house.

Kyle sat at the table beside them, and watched them. He said nothing about his visit to the courthouse.

That night, when Kyle left the store and started for the livery stable, Sheriff Jepson came across the street and intercepted him accidentally on purpose.

Tersely, he said, "I served my paper and then dropped in on the Minnifee ranch, the Box M.

Minnifee lives by himself, and there has been nobody holing up with him. They was no signs whatever of any visitor. I've been chasing outlaws for a long time, and I ought to know."

"Breathitt's been foolin' sheriffs for a long time, too," said Kyle. "You been hornswoggled."

"It wouldn't be the first time," said the sheriff. "But I simply don't believe it. Now let me tell you something. Gaynor's mighty spooky these days, and you could get yourself hurt bad. You better forget the whole idea."

That was Tuesday. Mr. Spencer was buried out at the S-Diamond on Thursday, and it was the next day, Friday, that Minnifee came into Gaynor and tossed his match into the powder keg.

Back of the Star Livery Barn, built onto its rear at a right angle, was a long, open-faced shed. Sometimes it housed a buckboard or two, or a carriage, in bad weather, and it had been erected for this purpose, but over the years it had become sort of a club room for outlying ranchers on visit to town. The proprietor of the stable moved out benches and a few cord-bottomed chairs, and it soon proved a favorite place for small stockmen to exchange gossip and friendships while waiting for their wives to finish shopping. Kyle, checking on Effie in the evenings, sometimes joined the group. Here he heard the sort of talk he enjoyed. As he was generally silent, and always courteous, he was instantly accepted.

Friday evening, after he had visited Effie in her stall, gone over her with his hands to see how she was being fed, talked to her softly to learn the condition of her nerves, he started for the shed outside, but halted at the stable's back doorway.

In the shed sat four dusty ranchers, all of whom Kyle knew by sight, and in front of them stood Minnifee, talking, bending toward them, gesturing emphatically. His audience was listening, hypnotized.

It seemed to be a private conversation, all right, but it was in a public place so Kyle wandered forward and joined them.

Minnifee gave him a fiery, baleful look and walked away. He walked directly into Kyle as he did it, and Kyle stepped calmly back to let him pass.

One of the ranchers turned to Kyle and said, "Did you hear that? Did you hear what Mr. Minnifee was saying?"

"I didn't catch the words," said Kyle. "But from the way he was carrying on, I figured he was candidating himself for something."

They didn't enjoy the lightness of his answer. They looked mighty grave.

"It's no joking matter," said a rancher with a wedge-shaped face and big, silky, waterfall moustache. "He said did we ever stop to think that maybe the Three L yearlings that's devourin' our grass, maybe they ain't even honest to start with. Could they be rustled cattle to start with, bought from thieves in the deep south, and brought here as a plague on us to exterminate our good Wyoming range?"

"What's his proof?" said Kyle, coldly furious.

"He didn't state it as a fact," said a third rancher. "He just said it could be an interesting thing for the ranchers hereabouts to speculate on."

Controlling his anger, Kyle said, "Do you think an outfit as important and high-class as Lowden, Lokely, and Lamont would do a lowdown thing like that?"

"Why not?" said the first speaker. "They're big enough to get away with it, like Mr. Minnifee says."

"Or look at it this way," said the rancher with the waterfall moustache. "Like I told Mr. Minnifee after we got to talking about it, it wouldn't have to be the company at all. It could be just Mr. Grinnell, running a rig on his bosses."

"And what did Mr. Minnifee say to that?" asked Kyle.

"He was mighty struck with it. He thought it over a minute, and said, 'By golly, you could be right. It would, or could explain how Walt Spencer got killed.'"

"Not to me, it don't," said Kyle.

"Walt Spencer grazed Three L cattle. Maybe someway he got to know too much about Grinnell's private operations."

"So Mr. Grinnell come over to Mr. Spencer's in the dark of the night," said Kyle "and shot him like a dog as he lay in his bed."

"Nobody said he did," said the man with the big moustache. "It's just that he could have. Like Mr. Minnifee said, it doesn't hurt to turn it over in your mind."

"I was raised up north," said Kyle. "On the edge of the Bear Paw Mountains. If we had meat, sow belly, once a week we was lucky that week. I had a little sister a year older than me, and we was so clothes-pore that sometimes she wore my clothes and I even wore her dresses like shirts. And I might add that nobody laughed at me, because they would be laughing at my maw, and my pa wouldn't have cared too much for that. We lived in a little shack with a dirt roof, and there wasn't nothing decent there but our thoughts and our talk. My pa said to us, 'When you grow up, and you listen to men talk loose, walk away.' Gentlemen, excuse me. And I doubt if you'll ever see me back here again."

It didn't humiliate them. It made them mad.

The first speaker said, "If we could get a look at Lochinvar's bills of sale from them cows we could soon tell."

"That's right," said Kyle woodenly. "Just go to him, and say you figure him for a thief, and ask to see them bills of sale."

They looked appalled.

"And I'd like to be present when you do," Kyle said.

He left the shed.

Back at the Red Front, Mr. Flake said cordially, "Have a nice walk? What have you been doing?"

"Just being friendly to one and all," said Kyle. "Making good customers for our store."

During the next few days, the rumor spread like wildfire. Some people discussed it laughingly, some skeptically, some quietly and earnestly, but everyone discussed it. And the more it spread, the more it was discussed, the more it seemed to pick up a sort of vague authority. There was something hypnotic and disturbing about the idea that those grass destroying yearlings at Three L might even be illegal to boot. The more it was talked about, the uglier it grew, the more some good people became unsettled.

And Minnifee was everywhere, making his oblique accusations, asking people to consider, conjecture, speculate.

Within a week, the county was divided into two nebulous factions, for and against. And Minnifee had become a man of importance, the spokesman for those against.

The story was late, naturally, in reaching Barbara, but eventually she heard it. One frosty morning she came to town, to the Red Front, angry and bewildered, to discuss it with her uncle and with Kyle.

While Melinda tended shop, the others talked it over in the upstairs privacy of Mr. Flake's bedroom.

"It can't be true, can it?" said Barbara. "That Mr. Grinnell killed my father?"

"Of course not," said Kyle bleakly. "Minnifee had him killed, and a man named Breathitt did it. Like I told you before."

"What's going to be done about it?" asked Barbara.

"That's hard to say," said Kyle. "Sheriff Jepson thinks nothing."

After a moment of deep thought, Mr. Flake said, "I don't understand it. Mr. Minnifee asking for open warfare with the Three L. If he ever really arouses them he'll be in serious trouble."

"Minnifee doesn't mind trouble," said Kyle. "Like a rattlesnake, a stupid lard-brained rattlesnake, he can't even scarcely feel it."

Barbara asked, "Does he really think he can whip the Three L?"

"He doesn't have to whip the Three L," said Kyle. "My guess is that he doesn't even care about that part, one way or the other."

"Then what on earth does he want?" asked Mr. Flake.

"He wants to stand up against the Three L," said Kyle. "This, just this, will make him big. He wants to go in little and come out big. Truth is, he's doing it. He's getting big already."

CHAPTER
FIVE

Tension in the town built up, and nerves continued to tighten.

When this thing cuts loose, Kyle thought, it's going to be awful. The thing about it was that people who could have no possible interest in it at all were growing excited, just excited. It was like a contagion they caught from their neighbors and friends. Now when Minnifee walked down the street, with his shoulder-gun, and thigh-gun, and bulky canvas jacket, he walked with a swagger, and people turned and looked at his back when he had passed. He was a personage.

Grinnell was a different story. He stayed away. You never saw him on Gaynor's streets. Kyle wondered why.

One morning, about ten o'clock, Kyle was in the post office getting Mr. Flake's mail. The post office was in Mrs. MacInnes' bakery, and he was standing by the window, eating a big doughnut, when a man stopped on the other side of the pane and motioned him outside. He didn't recognize the man at first, then he saw it was the wispy cowboy named Green River who worked for Three L and had befriended him that day out at their ranch.

When Kyle joined him, Green River began talking as though there had been no interval at all in the last time they had met. He said, "I just seen something that didn't give me no pleasure at all. Come along with me."

They walked a half block down Main Street. As they approached an alley-mouth, Green River said, "Take a quick look down this alley, then look away."

They passed the alley, Kyle looked in, then looked away.

What he had seen was Minnifee and another man leaning side by side up against a wall, chatting amiably. The other man was elderly, runty, but stocky and bull-like. He wore spectacles with crescent lenses. From his clothes, Kyle took him to be a small-time rancher, but he was incredibly, inexcusably dirty. He was in the act of taking a pint of whiskey from his hip pocket and offering it to Minnifee. Minnifee, all teeth and sociability, was in the act of accepting it.

"Worse than I thought," said Green River. "He's giving Minnifee the whiskey. *He's* doing the treating."

"Who is he?" said Kyle.

"A small rancher from out in the Turtle Creek country, named Delphy."

"Excepting that he's so filthy, what's wrong with him?"

"They ain't no more renegade Indians and outlaws, so to speak, and it's wormwood and gall to his dear old, silver-furred head."

Green River explained. Twenty or so years ago, in the really bad old days, the county was mighty dangerous. Outlaws and war-party Indians looting and raiding and murdering as the fancy took them. There wasn't enough law even to begin to handle it. Ranchers lived in worry, and their women lived in terror. Then a group of small outlying ranchers got together to stamp it out. They became known as the Turtle Creek Rangers. Green River was a boy down in Texas at the time, but he had heard the story locally over and over.

The Turtle Creek Rangers had stamped out the terror, all right. They became famous in three states. In Gaynor, they were heroes. But when the outlaws were under control, the renegades gone, and law and order restored, they couldn't bring themselves to let go of their power. They continued holding their secret councils, and judging community offenses, now for the most part trivial, way out of proportion. "That's the trouble with ambushes and rope-hangings," said Green River. "They can get like a disease."

Public pressure grew so strong against them, they disbanded.

"Disbanded," said Green River. "But a few of them now, still remembering those days of hard ridin' and power, keep mighty restless."

Brooding, Kyle rolled a brown paper cigarette. These old men, these ghosts, these leftovers from the Turtle Creek Rangers, could be just what Minnifee was looking for. A ready-made group to stand behind him.

Kyle said, "This could be the worse thing yet."

"Out at Lochinvar, we hear he's been wooing them for some time," said Green River. "But we hear, too, that he's only been partly successful."

"I'd say he was successful with Delphy," said Kyle.

"Yes, and Delphy, they say, was one of the worst."

When Kyle didn't answer, Green River said, "And look at it this way. If Delphy's in, maybe others will go in, too."

As they parted at a street corner, Green River said, "You're here in town. You listen to people when they talk. If you hear anything important, would you ride out to the Three L and let us know?"

"No," said Kyle. "I'd do it for you, of course, but I won't do it for Lochinvar. I'm not going to get mixed up in this thing."

But even as he spoke he knew he wasn't fooling himself. He was already mixed up in it, and plenty.

That night in his bed, the picture of Minnifee and Delphy drinking together in the alley stayed in his mind. Sleep came hard. When something like this came to a county, a lot of innocent people were always hurt.

Next morning, Sunday, he put on his gun belt and headed for the Minnifee ranch, to have a look around for Breathitt. Delphy and his Rangers might come or go, but Breathitt was Minnifee's standby, his scourge. He was being in secret reserve. Kyle was certain of that. What did Minnifee's swagger on Main Street add up to? It added up to Breathitt, hidden in reserve.

Sunday should be a good day to look the place over. Minnifee, enjoying his sudden spotlight, should be in Gaynor, exhibiting himself in church.

Breathitt had to be on, or near, the Minnifee ranch. He simply had to be. When you came right down to it, Minnifee was a general with a one man army. He was working like a beaver, trying to recruit others, but that didn't alter the situation. It was Breathitt he depended on.

He had no trouble finding Box M, Minnifee's spread. He had heard it much discussed. It was not far east of town, and he reached it a little after eleven o'clock.

This was mighty poor country, the sorriest he had seen around Gaynor so far; spotty scrub, thin grass, hard bare earth, even. When he first saw the ranch house, he brought Effie to a halt some distance away and looked things over. There was a corral at the side of the house, and Minnifee's big cinnamon mare was missing. Kyle was certain it had taken its master to town. He approached, dismounted before the front door, and called, "Anybody home? Anybody home?" He got no answer.

The house was a chubby little one-room cabin, its logs chinked with cow manure. Kyle opened its door and entered.

When you saw Minnifee in town he was always clean and neat, almost fastidious, but his living quarters were a different story. The place wasn't just dirty — you'd expect a bachelor to live a little messy — it was foul. Dirty clothes on the split-log floor, dirty clothes hanging from pegs on the wall, a table with food leftovers, a rumpled bed. Kyle started his search.

There were two chairs at the table, and two unwashed bowls with the remains of breakfast in them, rice and raisins. There had been a visitor here, but it could have been anyone, it could have been Delphy.

50

Kyle turned to the bed and went through it. Two greasy brown army blankets, and beneath them a homemade mattress, a cloth sack of dried sweetgrass. And bedbugs. Everywhere. However, they didn't impress Kyle one way or the other. Bedbugs were a cabin curse. The cleanest housewife could have them. He stood for a moment in thought. There was nothing here. Only that extra bowl on the table, and that could be harmless.

When he was sure everything was precisely as he had found it, he went outside.

Systematically, he searched the outbuildings, sheds, barn, blacksmith hut. If there was anything the slightest bit out of line, he couldn't see it. And he really looked.

A few yards to the side of the barn was the windmill. It was a direct-stroke mill, handy not only for pumping but also for sawing and grinding grain, and had once been a pretty nice piece of equipment. It was high, about forty-five feet, maybe. Some places, Kyle had heard, they rose to almost a hundred. Up its skeletal strip-steel sides ran a steel ladder. High overhead was the platform around the wind-wheel and its vanes. Though the idea seem ridiculous, it was the only thing Kyle hadn't searched, so he started up the ladder.

When he reached the top and stood on the platform it was like being in a different world. A noisy world, with the clanging and churning of the pump-rod and the rattling of the metal vanes almost in his face. And a thin, windy world, with distance below him stretching out on every side, to a misty, dusty horizon.

To east, south, and west lay the sorry range with its sparse scattering of miserable cattle. There was a strip of this range to the north also, but beyond it, in the near distance, lay a wild, matted, cedar brake.

It was then that he happened to glance at the floor of the platform on which he stood. In an angle between two steel plates was a handful of cigarette stubs. He counted them, fourteen. Slowly, he smiled.

You could look at it two ways. You could say that whenever Minnifee felt the urge to smoke a cigarette he came up on this uncomfortable platform to do it.

Or you could say that some person, persistently, had used this high perch as a lookout post. All things considered, that almost had to be Breathitt.

Kyle returned to town.

One thing about a tough town like Gaynor, Sunday on Main Street was sinister, and showed it. The rank and file of citizens stayed in their homes, off the walks, and left the town to the hard-cases. Kyle had stabled his mare, and was walking back to the Red Front. As he passed the open doors of the Mecca Saloon, he heard a loud voice coming from within, and stopped. The voice was Mr. Grinnell's. For the first time since the rumor had started, Mr. Grinnell had come to town.

The Mecca Saloon. Kyle shook his head wryly. He wondered how many Mecca Saloons he had seen in his day. If a town was big enough for three men to drink together, or for one to drink alone for that matter, it had a Mecca Saloon. He stepped inside.

He had never been in it before. Since he had had this town-job with the Flakes he had stayed out of saloons and started saving his money, just to see how it would feel. It felt pretty good.

The room was boxlike and big, with tables and a long, black-varnished bar. On the wall behind the bar, a brass key had been nailed to the wall with fence staples. Beside it, a sign said, *We Never Close*. In front of the bar were a few half-drunk cowboys and alcoholic citizens, standing in a circle before Mr. Grinnell, listening to him as he talked.

Mr. Grinnell, conversing with the group, was so cold sober himself that it was somehow almost like he was taking advantage of them someway. They were listening avidly, and he was speaking very deliberately.

His manner was haughty, and a little too overbearing for Kyle's taste. He was an important man, but an important man lots of times didn't waste his time acting important.

The bartender said effusively, "Mighty glad to see you around, sir. Some folks has wondered if you'd gone back East, or been transferred." His words were sly and probing, but his voice was bland and expressionless.

Mr. Grinnell was happy to respond. With great disdain, he said, "I work at Lochinvar, not at the Mecca Saloon. My proper place is where I work."

The bartender said, "Naturally, naturally."

One of the cowboys, hostile, said hoarsely, "Gaynor sees Minnifee 'most everyday."

"Lucky Mr. Minnifee," said Grinnell. "The fewer your cows, the greater your leisure." He took a small sip, a very small sip from his glass of beer, and added, "Any more questions?"

He managed to get intolerable contempt into his voice.

They gazed at him, and Kyle, with interest, saw that almost to a man they were unfriendly.

One of the cowboys, red-faced and daring, said brazenly, "Where did you get them yearlings?"

"In Texas."

"How?"

"I bought them, I believe."

"From a rustler?" asked the cowboy.

And Kyle realized a strange thing, which didn't seem to occur to the others. Mr. Grinnell had been playing for this very answer. The cowboy had been led along until he had said one word too many.

After an interval of deadly silence, Mr. Grinnell said, "Are you calling me a thief?"

"No," said the cowboy, alarmed at his drunken excess. "I'm just saying what I hear."

"Hear from whom?" asked Grinnell, and there was soft doom in his words.

"From Mr. Minnifee," said the cowboy.

Now Kyle understood the whole thing. These men and their remarks had been putty under Grinnell's hands. That was why he had come here, to trick them to put it into words, publicly.

Grinnell never did anything impulsively, Kyle was sure. He had made a decision and had come into town tonight to carry out its first stage. What was that plan?

Or when you came right down to it, why the first stage? Why not the second, or third stage, say? Possibly the others had been hidden and the plan was already well along in its execution.

Grinnell said, "If Mr. Minnifee wishes to question my honesty, why doesn't he look me up and say as much to me? I'm easy to find. Now, if you'll pardon me. I think I'll drop around to the Eagle Bar."

What he had done, Kyle decided, was right and natural. He had faced down a bad rumor. But he had done it in a scurvy way, trapping a half-drunk cowboy.

Grimly, Kyle watched him leave. He'd never look the same to Kyle.

The following afternoon, when business was at a lull, Green River came into the Red Front to buy a bottle of Neats' foot oil for a pair of stiff boots. Melinda waited on him, and after he had thrust his purchase in his pocket, he asked Kyle to step outside with him a moment. Kyle nodded and followed him.

Now and then, in the days past, Kyle had picked up quite a lot of information about him. He was all bones and tight skin. He smiled a lot, which Kyle usually considered a bad sign; but with Green River it was just something to do with his muscles while his mind raced on, trying to out-think you. Actually, he was quite a human. Out at the Lochinvar he was a top cowhand, the chief blacksmith, tallyman, and general factotum. Kyle had a deep respect for him, almost an affection. With the exception of the Flakes, and Barbara, it had before always taken Kyle about eight years to form an affection.

Now, Green River wasn't smiling. He was silent, too, and constrained.

Kyle, worried, said, "What's the matter with you? You sick?"

Green River spat on the boardwalk and said, "Right."

Kyle said, "What's wrong?"

"You'll see," said Green River.

Three horsemen came down Main Street, joined them at the edge of the walk, and one of them said, "Ready to go back to the Three L, Green River?"

"As soon as I get my horse," said Green River mildly.

They were dressed like cowhands and their clothes and saddles had seen a lot of wear and riding. Each man had a different model and caliber gun, one a Remington Army .44–40, one a Colt .45, one a Merwin and Hulbert .38; which showed quite a diversity of personal taste. They sat their saddles scornfully and were as vicious and ugly-looking a trio as you'd ever set eyes on. One, spiderlike, was all big chest and little bowlegs. One had the intense dead-looking eyes of a lynx. The other, apparently the leader, was prematurely bald, with his crumpled, flat crowned hat on his shoulders behind him, on its thong neck-cord.

Kyle, who had seen their like many times before, instantly put them down as mercenary gunmen, topnotchers, of the most brutal type.

Very cautiously, Green River made all-around introductions. "Mr. Hollister, Mr. Wheaton, Mr. Baldridge. This here is Mr. Fentress."

They didn't even look like anyone had spoken.

"You gentlemen out at the Three L?" asked Kyle.

"You goin', Green River?" asked Hollister. "Let's move."

Green River said, "Yes, Mr. Fentress. These gentlemen are out at the Lochinvar. They came yesterday morning."

Yesterday morning. They had been there when Grinnell had appeared in the Mecca last night.

Kyle nodded politely, and went inside.

These three men didn't arrive in the community simply to *protect* Lochinvar, Kyle decided. You didn't hire men like them for defensive measures. These men were here for offensive purposes.

Grinnell had crossed the line. He had swung into action. From now on, in town and country, it was going to be dog eat dog.

The bad trouble was here.

CHAPTER
SIX

The news came into town early next morning, and by noon Gaynor was boiling with shock and righteous indignation.

During the night, marauders had tried to burn out Delphy.

Delphy himself, ash-smeared and exhausted, came in about nine and gave the details. It had happened about three o'clock. He had been awakened by a gunshot and had opened his cabin door to see a mounted man a short distance off, sitting his saddle rifle in hand, while off to one side other men, maybe one, or two, or three, were torching his sheds and outbuildings.

He had taken a step into the open and the man on the horse had fired another shot. Delphy then had withdrawn again into his cabin and barred the door.

Soon, through the window, the sky seethed with scarlet flame and billowy black smoke. Delphy sat on his bed and listened to the crackle of his burning property. "I didn't have no lamp lit," he said. "And, by golly, I sure didn't need one. The light through the window was as bright and pink as a summer's morn." He said this over and over, and always added, "I could see that the mousetrap in the corner across the floor from me needed a new piece of bacon rind."

It was the cold-blooded way that it had been done that seemed so barbaric to everyone. How the men had wakened Delphy up so that he would be sure to see it, and then had savagely held him helpless, a prisoner, while they had done it. Gaynor put it down as one of the worst outrages it had ever heard about.

The sheriff had been out of town over the night before, and returned about one o'clock. As soon as he heard of it, he looked Kyle up and asked him to ride out to the Delphy place with him.

"Me?" said Kyle. "Why?"

"I jest thought you might like the ride," said the sheriff, beaming.

The Delphy place was not a ranch. It had once been a small farm, but over the years farming had become too humdrum for Delphy, the sheriff explained on the way, and Delphy had slid into a less laborious way of life. "Hunting, trapping, and fishing," the sheriff said. Then with surprising frankness, he had added, "And some says a little pilfering of neighbors when the moon is in the black. He's came a long, long way from the early days of them Turtle Creek Rangers."

"I put him down as a mighty dangerous old man," said Kyle. "Without an ounce of good in him."

"Every man has at least an ounce of good in him," said the sheriff reprovingly.

"You learn that by experience?"

"Well, no. I learned it at my mother's knee and it's so pretty I ain't never forgot it."

59

"I've never heard any talk of a Mrs. Delphy," said Kyle.

"There isn't any Mrs. Delphy, not any more. When she got tired of plowing and clearing new ground, she went and died on him, like an old ingrate."

The farmhouse, when they came up to it, proved to be a two-room shack with a dirt-and-stick chimney. Some distance to its left were the charred, smoky embers of what had once been outbuildings. A little group of men was staring fixidly at these embers. Kyle recognized Delphy and Minnifee. "The other three," whispered the sheriff as they approached, "are neighbors of Delphy's, old Turtle Creek Rangers, too." Everyone seemed in a rage.

Sheriff Jepson and Kyle joined the group and dismounted.

Minnifee attempted to take charge. First he pointed to the ground roundabout. For a hundred yards and more, the grass fire which had followed the burning had left the earth mottled with fluffy blackened ash. "No sign left *here*," said Minnifee. "The grass caught after they left."

The sheriff opened his mouth to speak, and Minnifee said, "So I cast around yonder —" he pointed in the distance, "for sign. Nothing there, either."

"Well, thank you, Mr. Minnifee," said the sheriff. "But I'll just take a look around, too."

He did, and found nothing.

When he returned to the others, he said, "This man you saw on the horse, Mr. Delphy. Just what did he look like?"

"I don't know," said Delphy brokenly. His face was still smeared with soot and ashes.

"Then," said the sheriff. "I don't guess there's nothing I can do. Right now, anyways."

Kyle expected them to explode in anger. They didn't. An exchange of glances went around the circle. They seemed satisfied.

"Don't give it a second thought," said Delphy. "Maybe somebody else will take care of it."

Sheriff Jepson made no answer.

Minnifee said, "There are two kinds of sheriffs, friends. One kind is mighty good at serving papers and suchlike. The other kind catches lawbreakers."

"Mr. Minnifee," said Sheriff Jepson placidly. "I never heard you talk like that to me before. I always had the highest regard for you. Do I hear you apologize?"

Kyle blinked. The whole scene was so relaxed, almost friendly.

Minnifee seemed to think it over. "Yes," he said, and his voice was like sandpaper.

"Yes, what?" said the sheriff, paternally, amiably.

"Yes, I apologize."

To Kyle, the sheriff said, "We'd better be getting back to town. If it suits you?"

"It suits me," said Kyle.

They mounted and rode away.

Back in town, the sheriff had a light, late noonday dinner at the Gaynor House diningroom, and asked Kyle to join him. Kyle had a cup of coffee with him. "This is the first food I've eat since yesterday noon," said the sheriff. "I been in the mountains west of here, trying to serve a homesteader with a bastardy paper."

"Did you get it served?"

"Well, yes. Finally." The sheriff turned over his hand and displayed its palm. There was a raw, deep cut. "He gave me a little tussle with his jackknife first. I guess that's why I was a little short tempered with Mr. Minnifee."

As the sheriff ate, and Kyle sipped his coffee, there was an irregular, almost constant procession of persons stopping by the table. Some chatted casually, some not so casually. The gist of all the talk came down to one thing. Lochinvar's three gunmen had Gaynor frightened.

If they would burn out Delphy, everyone said, who and what would be next?

Finally, when they were alone, and the sheriff had finished his meal and piled his tableware neatly in the center of his empty plate, Kyle said, "You know, when we were out to the Delphy place, and you was out looking for horse tracks and the others were staring at them smokin' embers, I sort of glanced at the front of the shack. Will you believe it, I couldn't seem to find any bullet holes like Mr. Delphy's story."

The sheriff became motionless.

Kyle said, "In my opinion, for whatever it's worth, Delphy set that fire himself, maybe helped by Minnifee, and that Breathitt I've been telling you about."

"Why? Why would a man do a thing like that?"

"To win over his old pals, the other ex-Turtle Creek Rangers."

"Who are these three Lochinvar gunmen?"

"You'll see," said Kyle. "But I can tell you right now, they didn't do it. It's not their style. If those animals had've had a hand in it, they would have burned the cabin, too, with Delphy in it. Wait until you get a good look at them."

They separated in front of the hotel, Sheriff Jepson heading for the courthouse, Kyle returning to the store.

There was a sidewalk bench for loafers in front of the Bluebird Barbershop, and as Kyle came near he saw it was being occupied by Green River who was using it more or less as a bed. The sun was full in his face, but he was sleeping on it, on his side, his hands under his jaw, his ankles hanging over its end. Kyle stopped, stood over him, and said in a harsh, deep voice, "I've warned you before, and I ain't going to warn you again. Stay way from my daughter!"

Green River opened his eyes slowly, swung his feet to the ground, stretched and yawned. He said, "Thanks. I was having a turrible dream. They was these six ugly bulls. They had me in a lonesome ravine, tied on the ground, and was fixing to brand me."

Kyle sat down beside him.

"And how," he said, "are your three new cowhands, Mr. Hollister, Mr. Wheaton, and Mr. Baldridge?"

"Not cowhands," said Green River. "Gunhands. If I didn't have such a good job, I'd move on. I don't know what got into Mr. Grinnell, setting them to burn out an old man. Even a mean old man like Delphy."

"I don't think they did it," said Kyle.

"Then you hold a different opinion from everybody else."

"That could well be," said Kyle. "But I ain't in the mood to go into it."

The afternoon was very quiet. Nowhere was there any movement except for the barber's bantam rooster out in the middle of the rutted road, working on a lump of horse dung, scratching, gobbling, scratching.

After a long pause, Green River said, "Kyle, tell me, what's going to happen?"

"Just about what I've seen happen other places," said Kyle gravely. "Ranchers killed on purpose, children killed by accident. And night riders."

"I know," said Green River.

"And in a way, the worst comes later. After the killing is over, the bad friendship lives on. For maybe fifty years."

Green River nodded.

Kyle said, "How are the other boys out at the Lochinvar taking the new visitors, Hollister, Wheaton, and Baldridge?"

"The funny thing," said Green River, "is that they're taking them fine. What with the Turtle Creek Rangers about to get together against us, they feel they could use a little professional protection. I hate to admit it, but I feel that way too."

"You should hate to admit it," said Kyle. "It could be I've met more of them kind of fellers than you have."

"One of them carries a toy gun, a .38."

"But I bet he could pick your teeth with it."

Green River said, "Why don't they leave us alone? What's wrong with a yearling eating grass? They got their own yearlings eating grass, haven't they?"

"The real trouble began," said Kyle, "when Minnifee started his story about Lochinvar being loaded with stolen cattle. It's that word 'stolen' that get people sizzling."

"But Mr. Grinnell disproved that in person. He came here in town yesterday, and made a tour of all the saloons, and faced them down on it."

"I know. I heard him at the Mecca. But he didn't disprove nothing, he just denied it. Matter of fact, he didn't even deny it. He just acted tough."

Green River said reproachfully, "You, too. You believe it, too."

"No, I believe it's a lie, because I believe Minnifee would naturally tell a lie. But when you come right down to it, it doesn't *have* to be a lie. You ever see them yearlings' bills of sale?"

"No," said Green River. "I'm just tallyman. I just count 'em on the range. They bring 'em to me, and I count 'em twice a year. Where they come from, and how they got there, I don't have no idea."

Now he suddenly seemed bothered. "You make me sick," he said.

"Well, don't take no credit for it," said Kyle. "You ain't the first one I ever made sick."

"I do believe I'll take a look at them bills of sale," said Green River.

"Does he keep them in his desk?"

"No, he keeps them in his safe."

"And, of course, you carry a key to the Lochinvar safe."

"Well, no. Not exactly. In fact, far from it. Nobody carries that key but Manager Grinnell. But I'm a mighty good blacksmith, and a reasonable locksmith, and that's a mighty old safe. I could make me a little piece of wire, with a twist at the end, and some dark night —"

Kyle got to his feet.

He said, "You'll do nothing of the kind," and walked away.

Barbara was in a buckboard before the Red Front, the reins in her hand; there were a few miscellaneous supplies on the floor by her feet. Through the store window Kyle could see Mrs. Spencer inside, packages under her arm, talking earnestly with Mr. Flake. Kyle, always sensitive about imposing on anyone, of taking advantage of a relationship, started to pass the girl when she said, "I'm Barbara Spencer. I live out at the S-Diamond. I don't mean to be forward, but you passed me without speaking and I'll get you fired. My uncle owns this store. Be average decent to me, and I might get you promoted."

Smiling, Kyle slowed down and halted. "Promoted to what?"

"You got me there," she said. "Blast it, all the important positions seemed to be filled, don't they?"

"I'm very happy where I am," said Kyle. He was so serious, it startled her.

"I'm very happy where I am," he said. "But I'd like to make a change."

Now she looked shocked. "You mean you want to leave Gaynor?"

"I like the Flakes, let's put it that way," he said. "But it's been bearing down on me that I ought to move out to the S-Diamond."

He studied her face, and she knew if she said the wrong thing she could wound him mortally.

"Well, I'll tell you one thing, I'd like to have you," she said honestly. "But why have you been worrying about it?"

"There's going to be a rain of blood in this country," he said quietly, certainly. "And you and your mother are alone out there."

"Who is going to bother a couple of harmless women?" she said. "They've already done their dirty work at the S-Diamond." Candidly, she added, "I think we're safer alone."

Now he was honest, too. "Maybe so. I would just taunt them, wouldn't I? But I fret about you a heap."

CHAPTER
SEVEN

It was later that day, in the early evening, when the Delphy thing happened.

Kyle had finished his supper, and was on his way to the livery barn to have his daily communion with Effie, when a half block down Main Street in front of him, Delphy came boiling wildly out of the door of the Eagle Bar onto the deserted boardwalk.

The old man turned, and came toward Kyle at a stumbling run. There was a four-inch welt under his eye, where someone had laid one on him, and his vicious old face was twisted in malignant fury. As he ran his head swiveled left and right, his eyes sweeping the ground for a weapon, any kind of a weapon. He wore a gun belt but there was no gun in his holster.

The way it looked to Kyle was that somebody had caught him no-show, had taken his gun from him, and slammed him around a little. Now, crazy mad, he was fixing to get even.

That was Kyle's thought at first, but instantly he knew better.

Two of the Lochinvar gunmen appeared from the doorway behind Delphy, grinning. The big-chested man with short bowlegs, Hollister, and the lynx-eyed one,

Wheaton. Wheaton held a gun belt, and tossed it into the road; they set out at a walk behind Delphy's running back.

Delphy wasn't running *to* anyone, he was running away from them.

Two doors toward Kyle from the Eagle Bar was a vacant lot. Delphy turned in, and, an instant later, Wheaton and Hollister turned in, too.

Now Kyle came to the lot, and stopped.

In that short interval, most of the work had been done.

The vacant lot, reaching from the boardwalk to an alley at the rear, was narrow. It was boxed in by shops on either side, a Furniture-Undertaker on the left, a hardware store on the right. Delphy, dazed, was on his hands and knees and the three Lochinvar men stood about him in a rough circle. Three. One of them had come down the alley. Delphy had been allowed to escape, just for the fun of catching him. The men stood motionless, in postures of action, like ball players frozen in mid-play.

Each held a gun in his hand, pistol-whip style, gun limp in palm, finger on trigger, in the true professional manner.

Delphy struggled, managed to get to his feet, and then they were at him, slapping his face with steel, wheeling him from man to man.

As Delphy made an arc of the circle, Kyle got a good look at his face. If you could call it a face. It was pulpy-red and half-toothless. Real pistol whipping wasn't just beating; it was as much a technique as quick-drawing.

"That'll be enough of that," said Kyle bleakly, forgetting he was unarmed.

"My opinion, too," said Hollister, smiling. "We're through."

Half dragging, half carrying, the three gunmen got Delphy's loose figure out of the vacant lot, down the walk to the Eagle Bar. A few people began to gather.

In front of the Eagle Bar was a farm wagon, its old mule tied to a hitching rack. Hollister taking one of Delphy's arms, Wheaton the other, Baldridge his feet, they tossed him into the empty wagon bed. "It's his'n, ain't it?" Wheaton asked the little gathering.

"That's right," volunteered a man in farmer's homespuns.

"Git in and drive him home," said Baldridge.

"I cain't," said the man politely. "You'll have to get someone else. I'm waiting for my brother while he gets his boot soled."

Baldridge took out a silver dollar, and handed it to the man. He didn't want to touch it, but was afraid to refuse it.

"Well, he's greedy enough for your money," said Wheaton.

The man climbed into the wagon seat, and picked up the reins.

Another bystander, a clerk in an alpaca coat, said, "Leave me call a doctor."

Delphy's lightless eyes were frosty and dull, and his breath came in feeble, mechanical wheezing.

"He don't need a doctor," said Wheaton.

Baldridge said, "He'll live."

"This time," said Hollister.

"You know something?" said Wheaton. "He's lucky."

"How is that?" asked Hollister.

"He's got a home to go to," said Wheaton. "When that bad fire hit him the other night, it burned just about everything but his home. I'd call it lucky it completely missed his house."

The farmer on the wagon seat snapped the reins and the mule moved down the street.

Hollister, Wheaton, and Baldridge went to their horses at the rack.

Rage simmered in the little group of citizens when they had gone. Rage and fear.

It was the fear they had been working for, Kyle knew. The rage didn't bother them. That was what brought them business, rage.

They had left Delphy alive as a frightening warning. They had brutalized him in retaliation, because they had been wrongly blamed for his burnings. Now outrages were coming fast, almost overlapping.

This was the true range war, Kyle knew.

Sometimes in range wars, on rare occasions, a large number of men had a shooting fight with another large number of men, but these fantastic occurrences were actually very rare indeed.

The true range war, for the most part, was a solitary man being bushwacked from a doorway. Or caught offguard, with the weight against him, and killed or severely injured.

It was here, had been here definitely for at least two days, and, like the others, would be harder to finish than it had been to start.

One thing Kyle suspected at the time, and became convinced of the next few days, was this. If Grinnell had actually given the order for the pistol-whipping, he had given a foolish order.

Immediately, it slapped back on him.

This, the people of Gaynor had witnessed with their own eyes.

It made them doubly sure these same three gunmen were, as they had suspected, the ones who had burnt out Delphy. Ill-concealed hostility against the Three L could be felt on every hand.

Before the end of the week, a half dozen of the old Turtle Creek Rangers were being seen on Gaynor's streets, and together. It was this being together that bothered a few of the town's old-timers, and brought a sour look to Sheriff Jepson.

By now, the sheriff and Kyle had become, well, sort of friends, Kyle realized. He didn't allow himself to realize it too clearly, because the idea seemed unnatural and alarmed him. He was forming mighty strange habits. Saving money, for instance. And palling up with strangers like the Flakes and Spencers.

And then, Delphy died.

Immediately, Minnifee began appearing in town with those hard-bitten old Rangers. No one was really surprised.

The bad part about it was that a lot of stupid people, who couldn't see any farther than their noses, nodded in satisfaction.

Investigation had proven, without a doubt, that, as crazy as it seemed, Delphy had started things that evening in the Eagle. He had picked an argument with Hollister (who, Kyle was sure, was just standing around ready), had brought in Wheaton and Baldridge, and the argument had moved into the first stage of the pistol-whipping. According to the free and easy justice of the peace there had been no real act of murder involved; Delphy had brought it on himself.

The sheriff did manage to get an assault and battery charge against the three men, though, and Mr. Grinnell paid out thirty-six dollars to the court, and bought the Eagle Bar a drink.

Everything was fixed up smooth as silk, but nobody was happy.

Mr. Spencer had been shot in his home, through his window, and no one had been arrested. Delphy's buildings had been burned, and Delphy same as murdered, and what had that amounted to? Nothing.

People openly, and scornfully, discussed who might be the next sheriff.

There were people who even wondered if it might be Mr. Minnifee. Whenever it was suggested to him, he would shake his head humorously and say, "I'm just a pore dumb cowboy."

It surprised him at first. But he never exactly said no.

Just when he was swinging his weight the most, Kyle had a little face to face with him.

It happened one afternoon when Kyle was in the barber chair at the Bluebird Barbershop, having his first real haircut in months, and it turned out later that

Minnifee had searched half of Main Street looking for him.

The inside of the Bluebird Barbershop was maybe twenty feet deep by eight feet wide. You sat on an oilcloth pad on a straight-backed kitchen chair, and faced across the narrow room. Along the wall you faced was a row of twisted-wire ice-cream-parlor chairs, with small, circular wooden seats, brass-rimmed, and here sat the customers, if any, and the loafers, always plenty. High on this wall, over their heads and directly opposite you, was an oval bedroom mirror, its silvered back tarnished and flaky. Unless you wanted to stare at a drunken loafer sleeping one off, you stared up at the mirror and watched the barber as he snipped at you. The place was vile with the smell of human urine from the rear, from the stink of encrusted spittoons, and from the barber's asafetida bag. Behind the barber was a low shelf made from a packing case containing lotions, tonics, razors and soap, and miscellaneous pocketknives, for he ran a cutlery-swapping business on the side.

He had just managed to douse Kyle's hair with lilac water, before Kyle could stop him, when Minnifee came striding in.

He was welcomed cordially by barbers, customers, and loafers. He wasn't welcomed at all by Kyle, who stared at him dead-faced, as though he were a medium sorry poker hand.

He said, "Fentress, eh?" and came over and stared down on him.

Kyle examined a back tooth with his tongue, and waited.

Minnifee said, "I'd like a word with you. Shall we step outside for a minute?"

"You mean right now?" said Kyle.

"Go right ahead," said the barber, affably.

"To hell with that," said Kyle mildly. "Finish up. What kind of a knothead is this, anyway?"

The room became a tableau of shocked attention.

After he had waited just a fraction too long, Minnifee walked from the shop. They could see him standing at exaggerated ease on the walk, his back to the window.

"Now I'm through," said the barber instantly, whipping his cloth in the air.

Wordlessly, Kyle stood up, paid him, and joined the rancher outside.

Minnifee said, "I'm going to ask you a question, and I want a straight answer."

"Choose your words a little better when you speak to me," said Kyle, blinking.

"No offense," said Minnifee. "Not yet, anyhow. I've been thinking about you. I may be wrong, but I think I know you, boy."

"I doubt it."

"Are you the same Kyle Fentress that was running wild over in Belle Fourche about five years ago?"

"I never run wild in my life."

"The boy I'm talking about was always in gun trouble, and always seemed somehow to come out ahead."

"I never throwed a gun in my life, in anger, or for pay."

"We're going to change that 'for pay'," said Minnifee. "We're getting together a little organization. And if you're the one I think you are, maybe we could use you. And not at a handyman's wages."

"Not me," said Kyle.

"You cheap, half-starved mongrel," said Minnifee. "We haven't even talked prices. You've heard the trouble here. Are you for me, or against me?"

"Get out of the way," said Kyle. "I'm going down the street."

The rear door of the Red Front opened onto an alley, and to the left of the door, inset into the backsides of neighboring buildings, was a well with a miniature roof to house it, and a wagon wheel as a windlass to its drum. This well served the little community near it; the Red Front depended on it for its water. Every night before Kyle undressed for bed, he took the chipped enamel dipper from its hook on the kitchen wall and went out into the dark little yard for a cold drink. He told himself this was healthy, and helped him sleep. He always drank the last drop in the dipper because he had been raised outside, where water was frequently precious. The idea of tossing the leftover water on the ground, as he had seen locals do, seemed to him criminal.

Tonight, about fifteen minutes of eleven, he had just drawn a dipperful and had it to his lips, when a hand came out of the dark behind him and laid itself on his shoulder. He spilled the whole works.

The hand belonged to Green River, and Green River seemed under a strain. He said, "Is there somewhere private we can talk?" and Kyle said, "Come inside."

They went in the back door, into Kyle's bedroom, and Green River sat on the bed.

Kyle looked at him. He was really on edge.

"Would you like a cup of coffee?" asked Kyle. "There's a pot in the kitchen, on the stove. It won't take long to heat it up."

"No coffee, thanks," said Green River. "I'm all right. Just give me a minute to catch holt of myself."

There was a moment of silence. Green River closed his eyes wearily, then opened them.

"What's got into you?" said Kyle. "Was it something you seen?"

"It sure was," said Green River, then lapsed back into silence.

"Am I supposed to guess?" said Kyle patiently. "Was it a monstrosity? Say a giant, man-eatin' frog?"

"Worse," said Green River. "A heap worse. I seen them bills of sale."

Kyle stared at him, speechless.

Green River said, "I made me my lockpick. Out of an old tablefork."

"Them bills of sale," said Kyle. "They was honest, wasn't they?"

"If you want to hear this, you leave me tell it my own way. I made me my lockpick. Last night, about midnight, I went to our office. Everything was dark —

office, bunkhouse, and Mr. Grinnell's little cottage nearby. I was facing the penitentiary, and I knowed it, but I was doing it for you, a friend, and went ahead."

"Get to the point."

"You leave me be! I knowed they always leave windows unlocked, and climbed in. I went to the safe an opened it with my tablefork."

"Didn't you have no light?"

"I climbed in the window, took a candle stub from my pocket, struck a lucifer and lighted it, went to the safe and opened it, as I said before."

"Listen," said Kyle. "You'll have to pardon me if I go to sleep. I had a hard day."

"I took out the bills of sale from the drawer in the tin box, and studied them keerfully in the candlelight. Ha, that got you, didn't it?"

"They was fakes, bogus?" Kyle shook his head. "I guess down in my heart I did really think Minnifee was right all along."

"Minnifee was a liar all along. Them bills of sale are perfectly legal. And certainly genuwine. Lochinvar cattle has all been properly bought, and from legal and honorable sources. The Texas notary seals they bear has to be authentic. I'm an old hand at this, and I'd swear them seals and bills is as good as gold."

There was a chill breath of coming winter in the bedroom, but Green River was sweating.

"Then what's troubling you?" asked Kyle.

"I ain't in the position to discuss it."

"Why in the hell not?" said Kyle, annoyed.

78

"It's a personal problem. It's something I got to take care of myself. In a way, I wish I'd never looked at 'em."

"At what?"

"At them bills of sale. What else are we talking about?"

Green River got to his feet. As he left the room, he said, "I sure don't relish what I got to do."

CHAPTER
EIGHT

The following day, Kyle got up an hour early. When he went out on Main Street, the street was empty. In an hour, clerks and shopowners would be busy sweeping off the board-walks before their places and bringing out sidewalk displays, ax handles in barrels, saddles, tables loaded with cheap shoes and dresses and chinaware. The air was crisp and sweet and the early sun was a fiery red lacquer against the store windows. When he came to a narrow doorless opening, slotlike, between a poolroom and a grain-and-feed office, he entered it and climbed dingy, splintered stairs to the second floor.

This brought him up into a bare hall, and, though it was dark here, he could sense shabbiness and disuse. He knocked on a door and his knuckles could feel the old scaley paint beneath them. A voice yelled, "Come in." He stepped inside.

This room, a long-abandoned lawyer's office with tall, thin windows overlooking Main Street, was now Sheriff Jepson's home. The sheriff, as he had once told Kyle, was not a man over-driven with earthly desires and the office was clean and tolerably weatherproof. It contained a bed, with a bear-skin rug before it on the floor, a table, a washstand, two chairs, and an immense pine armoire. The sheriff, in long underwear, wrinkled and sagging and fuzzy, sat on the edge of the bed. He arose formally, courteously, offered Kyle (who refused it) a chew of tobacco, took one himself, explaining it was a day-starting habit he had formed when he was about six years old.

He then gestured Kyle into a chair, selected one himself, and sat down. "Nice morning," he said conversationally.

"I'm sorry I'm here so early," said Kyle.

"Is it early?" said the sheriff. "I didn't notice. My watch is over at the jailhouse in a cell. I loaned it to a nervous prisoner."

After a genial pause, Kyle said, "There are some things you ought to know."

"A lot of things," said the sheriff. "Over the years, I've noticed it myself."

Speaking very carefully, wondering how the sheriff would take it, trusting to his friendship, Kyle told him how Green River had opened the Lochinvar safe, and about the bills of sale. It was a rough experience for Kyle. He had trusted few people, even in trivial things, and now he was confessing to the law about complicity in a safe opening.

The sheriff passed this point by completely. In fact, he seemed not to even hear it.

He said, "So the bills of sale were okay?"

"That's what Green River claimed."

"I'd sure take his word for it. But they bothered him?"

"My guess is, that they scared him."

"Well, it don't make no sense to me," said the sheriff. "But it tells me one thing."

"What?"

"If my office safe ever gets jammed, I'll get you to get some friend of your'n to open it for me."

The sheriff smiled gently, but Kyle didn't think it was funny.

Kyle then told the sheriff about his visit to the Box M, his search of the house, and the cigarette stubs on the windmill tower.

The search of the house was illegal entry, or at least trespassing, but the sheriff simply said, "Them cigarette ends doesn't have to mean this Breathitt you're always talking about. They could have got up there lots of ways."

"Name one."

"What about crows?" he said triumphantly. His voice was bantering, but his eyes were serious, clouded with deep thought.

Kyle then went through the worst ordeal of all. He told him about Minnifee's offer to hire him as a gun thrower. Only once since he had been in town, in a careless moment to Melinda, had he mentioned his borderline past. He had had a lightning reputation in those days, and in those days he had been proud of it. Now he wasn't so sure whether he was proud of it or not.

This point, the sheriff didn't let pass. He didn't let his real feelings, whatever they were, come to the surface. He merely said, "You look it, and I wondered, but I didn't believe it."

"That was five years ago," said Kyle. "I was only seventeen. And I never went on the gun, like they say. I mean as a trade. Lousey old cows are my trade."

A funny thing came into the room, a sensation they both acknowledged, that linked them together as close as blood, closer. The sheriff knew how Kyle had broken his lifelong code, three times, because he liked and trusted him. And Kyle knew that to this man he was completely okay.

"I'd better be getting back to the store," said Kyle, embarrassed. "How's all this going to stop, Sheriff?"

"I'm working on that problem right now," said the sheriff, benevolently.

By now, Kyle knew that when the sheriff looked benevolent, he was meaner than poison deep inside.

He had hardly stepped in the door of the Red Front when Melinda came forward to meet him.

He could hardly believe when he looked at her now that she was the same nervous, hostile girl that she had been when he had first come. And he understood the change in her. In fact, he was probably the only person she knew who could really understand this change. When he had first seen her, her mother had died and, without realizing it, she felt unprotected and helpless in the face of the world. Alone. Loneliness, Kyle could understand. He had been alone, really alone, most of his life.

First Melinda had learned to trust him, and then depend on him. She would never have admitted it, but he was like a brother to her now.

She said, "That nice little cowboy from the Lochinvar, the short thin one they call Green River, was in looking for you."

"Already this morning?" said Kyle, vaguely disturbed. "So early?"

"He talked quiet enough, but I think he was mighty excited about something," she said. Kyle believed her; she was almost intuitive about such things. "And he must have left the Lochinvar in a rush. His vest was buttoned crooked, and he wasn't shaved."

"What did he want?" said Kyle. "What did he say?"

Suddenly, to his surprise, the girl looked stubborn. "I don't think I'll tell you."

Kyle waited. He didn't try to force her.

"I don't know what it's all about," she said. "But it has to be trouble for you. He hasn't any right to draw you into something, whatever it is, and get you hurt."

He gave her a dry, reassuring smile, and she said, "He wants you to meet him at Johnson's place."

"As long as I've been in Gaynor," said Kyle. "I've never heard of Johnson's place."

"He should have said, Johnson's Rooms. That's what people around here generally call it."

"Never heard of that, either."

She pulled down the corners of her mouth. "Just as good you haven't. This Johnson is a bright-eyed, sincere-talking character who runs a faro game at the end of the downstairs hall in the Stockmen's Rest Hotel. Everybody thinks he's honest but me. I think he's as crooked as a dog's hind leg. They say he runs killer games. That he won't bother to accommodate you unless there's money, big money, involved."

When Kyle made no answer, she asked, "What could he be wanting there?"

"That's hard to say," said Kyle. "But it sure ain't gambling."

"Maybe Mr. Johnson is a friend of his?"

"I doubt it," said Kyle. "The way you describe him. Green River is honest to the core, and wouldn't have the time of day for a blackleg."

On a hunch, as he started to leave, he said, "Melinda, do me a favor. Don't pass this on to anyone, anyone at all."

Gravely, she nodded.

He knew wild horses couldn't drag it from her now.

He said softly, "You're all right," and went out the door.

He had hardly left the store, and started down the street toward the Stockmen's Rest, when he noticed a funny thing. About a block in front of him coming down the boardwalk was Mr. Grinnell, glossy and immaculate, and important-looking, swaggering a little, with a big smile and a cordial hand wave to just about everyone he passed. Farther down the walk, about a hundred yards behind him, came his three gunmen. They were talking and joking among themselves, seeming unaware of their boss, in a different world almost. But the funny part about it was that as Grinnell progressed he paused to speak briefly with people he passed, and always the men behind him slowed down a little to regulate the space that separated them. It sure looked like they were following him on a job. That they had been placed there by him on orders.

When Grinnell came to Kyle, he halted. Down the walk, the gunmen halted, too, apparently absorbed in their own conversation.

"Why, Mr. Fentress," said Grinnell. "Good morning. Howdy." He frowned unhappily. "I'm in a hole. Do you know anything about blacksmithing?"

"A little," said Kyle politely. "But I'm busy."

"We have an emergency out at Lochinvar," said Grinnell. "I'm in town looking for a good smith. Our straddle-row, two-horse cultivator has showed up with a split gear."

"That's a steel-welding job," said Kyle. "And I wouldn't be handy enough for that anyway. The best way, I'd say, would be to get a new one."

"I like to keep down expenses."

"Why do you call it an emergency? You won't be using it for months."

"I like everything shipshape for spring."

"Then why don't Green River fix it?" asked Kyle blandly.

"I don't know where he is," said Grinnell. "He seems to be taking the day off, all on his own."

"That ain't no way for a hand to do," said Kyle primly. "But he does work pretty hard, don't he?"

"You're a good friend of his, aren't you?"

"Did he say that? That was nice of him. Yes, I guess it's true."

"I understand he looked you up this morning."

"Not me."

"He was seen going into the Red Front. What did he talk about?"

"He came there, all right. For a hickory shirt, they tell me. I wasn't in, myself. I was out in the town."

"Then you haven't talked to him at all today?"

"Nope."

Kyle, in his answer here, was mighty painstaking to be careless in his response — but not too careless. Kyle had a feeling that this was a mighty important question to Grinnell.

Grinnell said, "I wonder where he could be. I've asked just about everywhere for him."

"He's probably sitting alone on a bench someplace," said Kyle, "eating peanut brittle or canned peaches. That would be like him. Enjoyin' life."

Without another word, Grinnell walked away.

Down the street, his three hirelings got into motion and started once more to follow him.

The Stockman's Rest was a white, slot-like building, rising two stories, with a narrow, double-decked veranda, the second-floor porch overhanging the sidewalk. It was quietly genteel, and catered mainly to the more prosperous type of old guard, from the outlying county. The other big hotel in town was the Central, mainly a railroad hotel. Kyle pushed open the door and entered a bare clean-smelling lobby. As he passed the desk wicket, he said, "Mr. Johnson," and a bespectacled clerk pointed to a door at the rear. He passed through it down a short hall, came to a door ajar and knocked.

A man opened the door, took him in with a glance, and waited. He was a well-dressed, boyish-looking man in his middle thirties maybe, with muscular dimples and a square cleft chin. He had a face that looked like it had been designed for honesty, but the important ingredient had been left out. This had to be Johnson, Kyle decided.

He said, "I was to meet a friend here."

"Not here," said Johnson. "These are my personal living quarters." He gave a flashing smile. "Maybe out front in the lobby, but not here."

Kyle said, "If you're Mr. Johnson, this is the place."

After a long moment, Johnson said, "Come in."

Kyle entered a small, tidy bedroom, surprisingly luxurious. There was a turkey-red rug on the floor, a mahogany bed with crisp, snowy sheets, a filuffy blanket folded across its foot, and a deep, cushioned chair by a table. A door across the rug was half-open and through it Kyle could partly see a second room, with a faro table.

Johnson stood and stared at him.

Suddenly, a strange conviction came over Kyle. In that moment at the door, Johnson, off guard, had told the truth. The whole thing was a mystery to him. Actually, he knew nothing whatever about any appointment here.

Something had gone wrong. What?

And why, if this was true, would Johnson invite him inside?

Kyle soon got the answer to his second question. Johnson had invited him in to pump him.

Gamblers were great gatherers of information. Information, almost any information, might be usable sometime or other. It might well be the edge, for instance, in a card-game crisis.

"Have a drink?" asked Johnson.

"No, thank you," said Kyle.

"Who were you supposed to meet here?" asked Johnson pleasantly.

"I don't know his name," said Kyle. "Fact is, I have never seen him."

"Then how would you recognize him?"

"I wouldn't. I was told he'd recognize me."

"Told by whom?" asked Johnson. It was beginning to bother him, and he showed it.

"I'm not at liberty to answer that."

"Why? I mean why were you to meet him here?"

"They didn't say," said Kyle. Then, just for the hell of it, because Johnson looked so pop-eyed and curious, he said, "If anything went wrong, I was to leave you a message."

"What message?" said Johnson.

"Eat, drink, and be merry, and watch your P's and Q's."

After a strained instant, Johnson, confused, said, "Was that message for me, or for your friend?"

"I wasn't told," said Kyle, and left.

Out in the lobby, he opened his mouth a little, and squinted his eyes. No sound came from him, but that was his way of laughing heartily.

Back again on Main Street, Kyle found the town churning with conversation. Dramatic news had just broken.

Mr. Grinnell had just announced that Green River was a decamping thief.

It had to be Green River, Grinnell had said everywhere. About ten thirty the previous night, the safe at the Lochinvar had been opened, and twenty-two hundred dollars had been stolen from it. Mr. Grinnell, himself, had seen the man as he left the office building. He had come out of his cottage for an evening cigar and a breath of air, and had seen him leave, in the bright moonlight. If it wasn't Green River, it was his double.

This morning Green River was gone from the ranch, and so was a Three L horse. That, the town decided, was proof enough for anybody, and twenty-two hundred dollars was twenty-two hundred dollars.

"Why?" Kyle asked a rancher. "Why didn't Grinnell say all this as soon as he hit town?"

Because he wanted to take care of it himself first, if he could.

Wherever Kyle could get an ear, he explained that it was impossible. That Green River was in his bedroom at the Red Front at that very time. Some people said he must be wrong, and ignored him. Others, figuring from his earnestness that he must be a friend, simply gave him a sympathetic smile.

A jury, he realized, would give him that very same smile.

CHAPTER
NINE

Sheriff Jepson was coming out of the little brown railroad station, and when he saw Kyle he made a diagonal across the wide road that intervened between them, and joined him on the boardwalk. It seemed to Kyle that he was the only one in town who wasn't wound up as tight as a spring. He said, "I just been to the depot, to see if a certain feller named Green River might have bought a ticket, say, to far, far away. He didn't."

When Kyle looked sour, the sheriff said quietly, "What do you make of all this new business?"

"He couldn't have did it," said Kyle, by now a little weary of the repetition. "Because he was with me at the Red Front, in my bedroom, at the very time Mr. Grinnell claims he saw him out at Lochinvar."

"I hear you been telling that story," said the sheriff in fatherly admonition. "Good pals should stick up for each other. But maybe it wouldn't hurt to stop it. Folks *could* get to wondering a little about you, too."

"It's about time folks get to wondering a little about Mr. Grinnell."

"The money's gone, Green River's gone, and a little blaze-face Three L mare named Angelina is gone, too."

He looked absently up and down the road. "And consider the horse alone. Stealing a horse in this country, from a big outfit like Lochinvar especially, ain't quite like filching a cracker from a cracker barrel."

"What have you got to prove Green River took that mare?"

"A witness. Angelina was seen in town this morning with Green River on her back, before the Red Front, I might add."

"Well, catch him and hang him. That would make you happy, wouldn't it?"

"It would make me happy to catch him, but I doubt if I would hang him. Unless he talked impudent to me, like you're doing."

Kyle grinned. "Excuse me."

Sheriff Jepson nodded. "Excuse acknowledged and accepted."

"Trouble with me," said Kyle. "I got into the habit of hard-talking around campfires and cook wagons."

"Then you're lucky you lived so long," said the sheriff, interested. "That's where I got into the habit of easy-talking. This is going to be a painful day on you, son. Be good."

He drifted down the street, ambling lazily, weaving through the excited citizens. People stopped him and asked him questions. He answered politely and briefly. He was the very picture of indecision, bewilderment, and incompetence. Kyle shook his head. For a long time he had been fooled, too.

He knew different now. This was a sheriff as smart as they made them, and all man.

Minnifee came riding down the middle of Main Street. He sat his big cinnamon like a swellhead. Like always, he seemed all guns. One badly concealed under his canvas jacket, one at his thigh. Kyle wondered suddenly if it wasn't deliberate with him. If he didn't want a hint of shouldergun to show.

In a knot close behind him rode three elderly men, also bristling with arms. They walked their mounts at a slow pace, that anyone who might so enjoy could look at them. They had no fifes or drums, but they were sure as hell on parade.

The funny thing was, nobody looked at them. People were too busy talking to each other about Green River. They passed out of sight, heading east.

Breathitt wasn't with them.

But Breathitt, he was sure, was around somewhere near.

Taking Minnifee into consideration, the kind of man he was, he had to be. Minnifee's hope was to get together as many troublemakers and sympathizers as he could, people like those ex-Rangers Kyle had just seen with him, but these would be as much for show as anything. Of course, it was convenient to have them and their weapons, if they were needed, but Minnifee wouldn't actually depend on them. They would be governed by whim; he would have no real control over them. They could side with him when they wanted to, and desert when the notion struck them. This, from Minnifee's point of view, would be too big an operation to put real bedrock reliance in them.

They weren't being paid. And Minnifee, from Kyle's experience with him, believed wholeheartedly in the power of cash.

He had without a doubt bought Breathitt, and Breathitt would do as he said, for that was Breathitt's livelihood.

So Breathitt had to be still around. The fact that he hadn't showed was understandable, too. Hiding and shooting, those would be Breathitt's great skills.

Kyle had had a little experience with each himself, and thought it over.

It was just a hunch, just a guess, but it was ten to one that he was holed up in that tangled cedar brake Kyle had seen from the windmill, just north of the Box M. Living like a savage, probably, spooky as a puma.

If this was so, it would be almost impossible for anyone to run him down.

Mr. Flake and Melinda were in the stockroom making inventory. They welcomed his appearance with deep, quiet friendship, but were so meticulous in the work before them that Kyle realized they were concerned for him. He figured he must be showing his mental distress. Hardly realizing what he was doing, he sat on the corner of a packing box and told them about his experiences on the street and with Johnson at the Stockmen's Rest.

Mr. Flake got into the conversation. He asked Melinda to repeat again, as accurately as she could, the message Green River had asked her to deliver to Kyle. She did. "It makes no sense to me whatever," said Mr. Flake. "It's hard for me to imagine Johnson fiddling with a poor cowboy like Green River at all. It's hard for me to conceive of Green River going there."

"That's what he said," declared Melinda.

"Well, Johnson didn't know anything about it, didn't expect him," said Kyle. "A good gambler has to be a good actor, and all of that, but I'm dead sure it was news to him. You should have seen him. He was completely sprangled."

"What do you think?" asked Mr. Flake.

Kyle said, "I think he was headed for there, if he said so, but something come up, maybe Grinnell, and sidetracked him."

"You think he's dead?" asked Mr. Flake.

"I doubt it," said Kyle. "I figure Green River to be one slippery onion, if he has to be."

For a moment, everyone was silent. Finally, Kyle said, "And right now he'd better be. Did you know him, really?"

"Only by sight and to speak to," said Mr. Flake.

"Well, I haven't knowed him long," said Kyle. "But a funny thing, I think I know him well. It's that way with you and some people. And if he hadn't even been here with me when they claimed he did it, I'd swear he was innocent."

"Then who was it that Mr. Grinnell saw coming out of his office?" asked Melinda. "The man who was a double to Green River?"

"Personally," said Kyle. "I didn't think Grinnell saw nobody."

This shocked them. Even Mr. Flake objected to it. "You mean Mr. Grinnell is spreading a bald-faced lie?"

"How can it be otherwise?" said Kyle. "I've told a thousand times that Green River and me was together. You can believe who you want to, me or him. I *know*."

Mr. Flake said quickly, "I didn't mean that. I just meant that maybe Mr. Grinnell made an honest mistake."

"But he did take a Lochinvar horse," said Melinda. "I saw it in front of the store this morning. I saw him mount it and ride away."

Patiently, Kyle explained. "All of a sudden, he's scared of Grinnell. He grabbed the horse to get long gone." Kyle got to his feet. "So let's don't talk about it anymore. It's getting to make me nervous."

"When I see you nervous," said Mr. Flake, "— about anything, it will be hard for me to believe. You've got nerves like steel. The real fact is that you're unhappy."

"The thing is," said Kyle, "because he carries a gun don't mean he has an idea how to use it. Jest like the rank and file of cowhands, he probably totes his forty-five as a tool. To put hurt horses out of their misery, for reptiles at water-holes, or maybe, like most of 'em, because he's took a fancy to its shiny barrel and stag handle. He could be so bad he wouldn't have a gunfighting chance with even Miss Melinda here."

"Oh, I hardly think so," said Melinda, shaking her head. "I don't like loud noises."

"You think he's in serious danger?" asked Mr. Flake. "And that he needs you?" Kyle nodded.

He walked to the door. In the doorway, as he left the room, he said, "That's exactly it. And I don't know what to do."

96

The little bell in the shop, just above the front door, tinkled. This meant there was a customer out front. Kyle said, "I'll get it."

It was Grinnell. He was standing by the millinery counter, listlessly tapping a sewn-leather English riding crop against his knee. His pop-eyes were glassy with a mixture of weariness and worry, and his black-broadcloth clothes were wrinkled and baggy. Kyle passed before him with no greeting, lowered a window shade about ten inches to cut a sunbeam off from a jar of chocolate drops, and then stood motionless, waiting to be addressed.

Finally, Grinnell said, "Some of the boys at Lochinvar think you and Green River must have been in this thing together."

Kyle looked stupidly uninterested.

"Do you care to deny it?"

"I don't care to even answer it."

Grinnell said, "The bunkhouse at Lochinvar, they tell me, is really buzzing. And it's you, mainly, they're talking about."

"Why?"

"They want that money back."

"Your cowhands? Why?"

"I've explained to them," said Grinnell, fastening his glazed eyes on Kyle, "that part of it was their payroll. Now they'll have to wait a little to get paid."

"This is something new," said Kyle, returning the stare. "you mean you won't pay your hands until Green River returns the money you're claiming he stole?"

"No, I didn't mean precisely that," said Grinnell. "I mean there will be an unavoidable delay. This is a serious thing. I'll have to get in touch with Boston, inform them of the situation, and ask for their go-ahead."

"Well, I never heard nothing so silly."

"I just want to do the right thing."

"You just want to foment up your Lochinvar hands agin me and Green River, you mean."

"Not at all," said Grinnell, showing the edge of his teeth in the slightest lifting of his upper lip. "Though I must admit that seems to be what's happening. So far I've been able to keep them under control."

Kyle started to walk away, then stopped. "Is that why you're here right now? To threaten me?"

"I'm here to ask you to co-operate."

"Just hand over twenty-two hundred dollars, and apologize. Is that it?"

"No," said Grinnell serenely. "I don't think you have it, or any part of it. Or haven't even seen it."

This was a surprise development. But the surprise soon straightened itself out.

Kyle said coldly, "You mean it didn't exist."

"Oh, it existed all right," said Grinnell, back again on the same old track. "But I mean Green River used you as a dupe. That you actually had nothing to do with it."

"Dupe, how?"

Grinnell paused, and got his words organized. "He was seen here this morning, on one of our stolen horses, incidentally. I figure it this way. He brought you the money, in an innocent package or bundle of some kind. You say you weren't here when he came, and I've verified this. So if he left it, the money, he'd have to leave some word of instruction, too. Say, for you to deliver it to him later in the day, at some particular place. You were seen going out right afterwards. Where did you go?"

Now Kyle saw how Grinnell had tried to build a vise of words around him. How this was the moment, how he was applying pressure, trying to get him to talk.

And if he knew this much, it would be like him to hold one more fact in reserve, to test the truth of Kyle's story.

Kyle said, "I went to the Stockmen's Rest."

"Why?"

"He asked me to deliver a funny message to Mr. Johnson."

"Message?" said Grinnell tensely. "Mr. Johnson? What was it?"

"I've forgot already," said Kyle, frowning. "You'll have to ask him."

"And don't think I won't," said Grinnell, striding to the door, venomously satisfied.

The next five hours passed without event. About four o'clock, when business was in a lull, Kyle left the store and made his way to the courthouse, to learn what was what.

At the courthouse they told him the sheriff was out with a search party. They told him, in fact, that there were five parties out combing the countryside, blindly. Minnifee and Grinnell and their range trouble seemed temporarily forgotten. There was nothing like the sensation of a so-called robbery, Kyle decided, to make people overlook their own personal danger. He wondered for an instant if Grinnell had invented the situation for this very reason, but decided no. He had invented it, all right, but his reason must be deeper, more cunning. In a couple of days this bogus robbery would be no longer of any interest to anyone, and Grinnell was a man who planned farther ahead than that.

When Kyle got back to the store, he found Barbara's sorrel tied to the rack outside, and inside, Barbara and Melinda and Mr. Flake were around the kitchen table. They were all mad, even Mr. Flake, who was always even tempered. Kyle felt the coffee pot on the stove, poured himself a cup of coffee, and brought it to the table. He thought he'd find them talking about Green River, but they weren't.

Barbara said, "And then he offered mother a twenty-dollar gold piece, and she turned her back. He said, 'That'll pay for it, that's the price it might bring at the chutes,' but she paid no attention."

"Who?" said Kyle. "For what? What are you talking about?"

When she told the story again, for his benefit, he got so angry he could hardly keep his face from showing it.

About noon that day, while Barbara and her mother had the big copper wash boiler going with its fire under it, and were washing clothes behind the barn, Mr. Minnifee and three men came riding up from the south range, driving a big fat Lochinvar two-year-old before them. She didn't know the other men to speak to, but she had seen them over the years, and had been told they were old Turtle Creek Rangers.

Mother Spencer put down the hickory ax handle she had been using to punch the clothes around in the boiler, and came forward. Sensing danger, but ignoring it, she said, "What are you going to do with that cow?"

One of the old Rangers, grinning through rotten teeth, said, "We're fixing to analyze it."

"But we're doing it to your face," said another. "Not behind your back."

Now Minnifee got into the conversation. He said coldly, "I don't like this any better than you do. I ain't accusing either of you two ladies of law-breaking, not you personally, but if you associate with thieves like Grinnell, and take pay from him, you got to expect things like this."

They all dismounted.

The cow started to walk away. One of the Rangers drew his .45 and shot it. It rolled to the ground, kicked a few times, and stilled in death.

"Did that make you any happier?" Barbara asked.

They pretended not to hear her. Minnifee unsheathed a skinning knife, bent over, and, after a little labor, peeled off a square of the still-warm hide, about a foot square.

The four intruders gathered around it, and examined its reverse side.

Barbara and her mother knew well what they were doing. A tampering with a cow's brand, a dishonest altering with a running iron, for instance, left its story on the inside of the hide.

"Find anything suspicious?" asked Barbara coldly.

"Nothing suspicious," said Minnifee. "But that don't mean nothing. Not that it couldn't have been stolen. Say it was rustled down in Texas, and moved quick out of the state, and not altered at all."

"But you were expecting a running iron, or at least pretending to expect one," said Barbara. "And didn't find it."

"Oh, we'll find one, all right," said Minnifee. "This hain't the only cow grazed by Lochinvar."

He took a twenty-dollar gold piece from his canvas jacket and held it out to Mrs. Spencer. She turned her back. "That'll pay for the cow," he said. "That's about the price it might bring at the chutes."

Faltering, he restored it to his pocket.

They swung into their saddles and rode away.

"The dead cow's still there," said Barbara. "Out there, on the ground behind the barn. I haven't told Mr. Grinnell yet."

"Somebody's got to stop this Minnifee," said Kyle softly. "He's going to keep at you as long as you people are connected with Lochinvar. You see why, don't you?"

When they didn't answer, he said, "He figures Mrs. Spencer and Barbara are just a little safer to go up against than Hollister and Wheaton and Baldridge."

"He's really a grub-worm, isn't he?" said Melinda.

"Yes," said Kyle agreeably. "I'm afraid he is."

After a bit, Barbara left to meet her mother at the hotel. Kyle, unable to speak to customers because of his anger, or even look at one, finally went into his bedroom.

He was sitting on his bed with his gun belt in his lap, simmering, trying to make up his mind whether to go out and look Minnifee up and maybe settle all this for good, but knowing it would be wrong, knowing that was what the law was for, when there was a light rap on his door. He put the gun belt under the bed clothes.

Hoarsely, he said, "Come in." Mr. Flake entered.

"Something just occurred to me." he sad.

"What?" asked Kyle, sensing something of importance.

"I could be wrong," said Mr. Flake. "But I could be right."

Kyle waited.

"This morning," said Mr. Flake, "when your friend Green River came in and talked to Melinda, maybe she got excited and partly misunderstood him."

"She must have," said Kyle. "But it's too late now." Quickly then, to cover for the girl, he added, "But anyone can mis-hear somebody."

"He said one thing, and she thought afterwards that he said another. Just now I asked her, and she says I could be right."

Kyle nodded patiently.

Mr. Flake said, "She thought he said Johnson's place, and he must have said 'the Johnson place'. They sound alike, but are quite different. Johnson, the gambler, is so well known around town, he would instantly come into her mind. The Johnson place is out in the county. I doubt if she ever heard of it before."

"I never did either," said Kyle. "What is it, a ranch?"

"It's an abandoned cabin. Johnson was one of the very early settlers here. He and his kin, no relation to

103

our present gambler, I might add, have been long gone from the community. They were gone, in fact, before I came."

Kyle stood up.

Mr. Flake said, "He could well be waiting for you there all day."

"Yes," said Kyle. "How do I find it?"

Mr. Flake told him.

"You'd better hurry," said Mr. Flake. "And don't get hurt."

"You mean you're really interested in this Green River?" asked Kyle.

"I'm interested in you," said Mr. Flake. "And your sense of honor to yourself."

When he had gone, Kyle put on his gun belt and went to the livery barn.

The day had started in bright golden sunlight, with cottony white-bottomed clouds against a brilliant crystal-blue sky. By noon, these clouds had moved away and a single, high-altitude cloud of sluggish gray, like a vaporous sheet of dirty muslin, had crept across the heavens from the southwest. The moisture started in mid-afternoon, seeming to come with no fall, but to simply materialize, and the town became slatey with drizzle. Now, as Kyle passed down Main Street, riding out of town, his shirt became soggy on his back. But though he owned a tattered India-rubber poncho, he left it behind him. When there was any possibility of gun play at all, he wanted no poncho fighting his draw.

104

He left town by its eastern pike. Dusk was falling and the country about him was fast becoming a murky half-world.

Just out of town, he found the slaughterhouse, where Mr. Flake had told him — where slaughterhouses generally were — and turned his mare from the pike, around it. Behind it he found the path, and bore along it, through scrubby grease-wood. There would be about three miles of this, Mr. Flake had said.

He moved with caution, for every square inch of the county could be battlefield these days.

There was one thing about all this that was hard for Kyle to understand. With all the hue and cry out for Green River, why had he come to the cabin? Sewing himself up this way, hiding out locally, could only make it harder for him to cross the prairies later. Today the search had been bad enough; tomorrow, when the word had really spread itself out through the country, and the town itself had become organized, it would be twice as hard for him to get away.

Looking at it that way, it seemed a stupid thing to do, hiding out so close to town. And Green River was a long way from being stupid.

For some reason, he seemed to be waiting for dark. But how could that help him? What Green River needed, it seemed to Kyle, was distance, not dark.

But all this was just guessing.

And then Kyle saw the cabin.

CHAPTER
TEN

Automatically, Kyle stopped and took his bearings. This was a lonesome place, yet scarcely three miles from town.

In the gray twilight, in the thin misty drizzle, the house stood lightless, a black hulk barely distinguishable from the wild, ancient cedars which engulfed it on all sides. He rode forward and dismounted, and saw instantly that it had been long abandoned.

It was a small cabin of unbarked logs, with a black, gaping window. Across its front wild vines, year after year, had sheathed its front in a tangle of tendrils, now dead and dripping in the moisture. Beside the door was the open maw of a vegetable cellar, now weed-choked. The door was gone, and the door frame was rotted and askew. Kyle stepped inside, and struck a match.

In the short minute of sulphurous light, he saw much. He saw the little log-walled room with its dirt floor, spongy from long disuse. He saw tracks in this dirt, hoof-prints as well as boot-prints; a horse and a man had been here, and for some time, as the prints were overlaid and plentiful. In a corner he saw a saddle with a Three L stencil on its skirt. There were horse droppings, too.

The match went out against his fingernails. He dropped it, stepped on it, and stooped to feel the horse dung. It was not warm, but it certainly was not cold either. It could be, say, two hours old.

Green River had been here, there was no doubt of that, and had gone.

But he'd gone without his saddle. And an old range hand like Green River would never ride barebacked if he was trying to make time. Which he certainly was.

Did someone supply him with a new horse and saddle? It wasn't likely.

What had happened, then?

There was a kind of cowboy, a long-distance mover, who when he drifted favored the railroad. He beat his way blind baggage, or on the rods. He liked to cover territory, and quick. He was a long way from being a hobo, but he knew the hobo tricks and life like the back of his hand.

This would explain everything and would fit Green River's character as Kyle had figured it.

Where, hereabouts, would be the best place for him to catch his hold? There was only one place, really — the yards coming out of Gaynor, before the locomotive had picked up speed. Out on the plains those contraptions really rolled.

Green River had come here, and hidden, and waited for night, so when men came to the yards he wouldn't be seen.

He'd kept his mare with him, and had then turned her loose as he himself left. She mustn't be found too quick. Now she wouldn't be seen until daylight, at least.

Another man might have left her tied up, inside this building, to die.

Right this minute, Kyle decided, Green River was just beyond the yards, just beyond the western fringes of town, waiting for a freight.

If he hadn't already caught one.

Kyle returned to Gaynor.

The drizzle had turned to rain, thin but chilly and pelting, when Kyle got into town. This could well be the forerunner of a cold snap, he decided. Because of the rain, Main Street was deserted. Shop lights glistened behind streaming windows as he passed, and made golden pools in the mirey road.

He followed the railroad tracks south. The houses and shops became sparse, the vacant lots increased, and finally he was out of town. Then he was walking Effie through the railroad yard.

The place Green River would select would be beyond the yards, a short distance on the yonder side. Where the trains would be moving, but not yet moving too fast.

As a railroad yard went, this one wasn't too big, but it was more than enough for Kyle. If there was anything that made him uneasy, deep in his heart — so deep he refused to admit it even to himself — it was a railroad yard. He didn't like any of it, the tracks, the locomotives, the baggage cars and passenger cars and freight cars. It all seemed so unnatural to him, and somehow ominous. He wove his way through the great wooden and steel hulks, glossy with rain, still now,

108

silent. And then they were behind him, and the rolling plains began.

He brought his mare to a halt, and looked around. There was no one in sight.

To the left of the tracks, about twenty feet back, was a salient of scrub, sumac and hazel. From deep within it came a watery crimson glow, about at ground level.

It had to be a camp fire. But a man on the dodge doesn't build a camp fire. And whoever built this one, really worked over it, for it was built in the rain.

He wondered if it was trap. Well, he thought, we'll see. He moved toward it.

In the thicket was a clearing, and in the center of the clearing was a small fire, skillfully built, and skillfully protected by a ragged poncho supported by dead branches. A man sat by the fire, drinking coffee from an old tomato can. It wasn't Green River, by a long shot. It was a rheumatic, depraved-looking hobo, wearing two coats and with a rope for a belt. Beside him, on the ground, was his bandana bundle of necessities. He gave Kyle a predatory look, appraising him financially, in detail, then dismissed him, and returned to his can of coffee. Kyle dismounted, and squatted beside him.

Because Kyle had a horse, the man knew this was no brother hobo.

"This ain't no public cafe," he said. "Move on."

Kyle tried to fix up a suitable story. "I'm meeting a friend here, a friend in trouble. You seen him?"

"No, Sheriff," said the hobo. "I ain't."

"Sheriff?" said Kyle, and laughed. This was the first time he'd ever been called sheriff. "You don't see a badge, do you?"

"I see a mighty well-cared-for sixgun," said the man. "The badge could be in your pocket."

Suddenly, Kyle had the chilly feeling that a man was standing behind him. Slowly, he turned.

It was Green River, grinning.

When the hobo saw Green River grin, he grinned a little himself, found another old can, and poured Kyle coffee. Kyle accepted it. Green River sat on his heels beside him. "No hard feelings," said the hobo. "I just had to be sure."

"No hard feelings," said Kyle, and drank. It was pretty good coffee.

"I didn't rob the Three L," said Green River. "And you and me both know it. When the robbery happened, I was sitting on your bed, at the Red Front with you."

"Of course," said Kyle. "I never thought you did."

The hobo said, "I can see this is personal. If I was the right kind of fellow, I'd get up and walk away so you could talk in private. But I'm the wrong kind of fellow, and got stiff joints, and like to eavesdrop, and got a weakness for listening to any kind of robbery talk."

"I got nothing secret to say," said Green River.

"Stop running," said Kyle. "Come back to Gaynor with me. And we'll discuss it with the sheriff."

"No."

"You afraid of the sheriff?" asked Kyle.

"I'm not afraid of a sheriff, or a cell, or stuffed jury," said Green River. "But I'm sure as heck afraid of twelve big bullets, fired in a volley at the rapid, coming so fast you can't hear no separate detonations."

"Who is aiming to do that to you?" said the hobo.

They ignored him.

"And a freight train will save you?" said Kyle.

"It'll get me someplace else. And that's where I want to be."

"When most animals hunt, they hunt silent," said Kyle. "Except the bobcat. He howls and makes all the roaring he can. You'd think his prey could take advantage of it, but they don't. You know why he's so noisy?"

"Yes," said Green River.

"Not me," said the hobo. "I've often wondered."

"A bobcat howls to scare his prey," said Kyle. "He likes to get them on the run. They're helpless then, and don't have all their wits about them. It's even worse with humans. A man on the run is open sport to any other man that wants to pull a trigger."

"You mean well, but you're wasting your time," said Green River. "This time next week I might be back in Phoenix, happily and safely mending parasols for ladies."

The first shot was a single explosion and it was this one, Kyle realized later, that killed Green River. The shots that followed came in a continuous deafening roar, like the thunderous ripping of a piece of cloth.

Green River was flung backward to the earth and three men came out of the darkness, into the feeble light of the fire, walking, firing as they came. They were intent, as though in target practice. Kyle had seen men shoot this way in amusement, at bottles floating down a creek stream.

They were the three gunmen from LLL, Wheaton, Baldridge and Hollister. There was a moment of silence.

They formed a little circle about Green River. Hollister bent and felt his pulse.

"Dead," he said.

"I wonder why?" said Kyle. "He was all right a minute ago."

Baldridge said, "He never knew what hit him. It was painless."

"Not to me," said Kyle mildly.

"You know something?" said the hobo blandly. "I didn't even see him when he went for his gun. It was almost like he was shot unawares."

"He was a robber," said Wheaton. "And you kill robbers like you kill snakes."

"What did he steal?" said Kyle.

"You know what he stole," said Wheaton. "The whole county knows. He stole twenty-two hundred dollars from the Three L."

"Well, that's that," said Wheaton. "Another job well done. All right, boys, let's go."

They started across the clearing.

Kyle said. "Aren't you going to search him?"

They stopped. Hollister said, "For what?"

"For the money," Kyle said.

"Of course we're going to search him," said Hollister. They returned to the body and made a busy, bogus search.

112

When they had finished, Kyle said, "What did you find?"

"Nothing," said Wheaton, pretending great disappointment.

"Which proves nothing at all," said Baldridge. "He must have buried it somewhere, to come back and get later."

They were enjoying the game. Suddenly, Wheaton said gravely, "An idee has jest come to me. Maybe he give it to a friend to hold for him — until he caught his freight. Mr. Fentress, you was a friend of his, wasn't you?"

"And still am," said Kyle.

Now all three of them were enlivened at the horseplay developing. "Just lift your arms, Mr. Fentress," said Wheaton. "I'm afraid we're goin' to have to undress you."

Kyle made not the slightest move. He said amiably, "The first man that makes a quick move has ate his last piece of chocolate cake."

They froze.

Kyle stood easy and relaxed, and studied them. They were mercenaries and that meant they were wizards with their weapons. Being mercenaries, they'd like it best shooting out of the dark, like they just did, but being men, too, they had their tempers like anyone else, and anything could happen. The big thing now, the electric thing, was their pride. What a hired gun had to merchandize, even more than his six pistol, was his reputation. And it was in situations like this, that jumped up unexpected, that his reputation could get punctured mighty quick.

Into the little clearing from the stillness of the night came the puffing and chugging of a distant locomotive, leaving the yards.

The hobo got to his feet. "That's my freight. I swear and declare I scarcely know how to make up my mind. This is awful. Shall I catch it, or shall I hang around?"

"You better catch it," said Kyle. "If they shoot me it'll be murder. Nobody accuses me of robbery. They won't want any witnesses. Likely, they'll shoot you, too."

The hobo arose and folded up his poncho. With surprising dignity, he left the thicket.

Beyond the brush, they could hear the train approach, hear it puff past, hear its sound diminish as it was swallowed by the lonesome, distant prairie.

Now the pelting rain was fast extinguishing the camp fire. Somehow, Kyle sensed the tenseness had eased.

"You should have grabbed a little of that freight yourself," said Wheaton, conversationally.

"Me?" said Kyle. "Why?"

"For one thing, you can't seem to mind your own business."

"Watch it, Jim," said Baldridge.

They were talking business now, Kyle felt. Their business was to kill on orders. They hadn't been ordered onto him. Not yet. But they sure expected to be, and before long.

First Minnifee on his back, and now Grinnell, too.

He took his mare by the bridle, and led her from the thicket.

CHAPTER
ELEVEN

The rain, when Kyle returned to Main Street, became suddenly fierce and lashing. Because of its density, the night lights behind the row of shop windows seemed weak and dim. There was no illumination from the sheriff's office in the courthouse as Kyle passed, taking his mare to the stable. As he returned on foot, however, he saw that a light had appeared in the interval. He crossed the muddy road, entered the building, and went down the stairs to the half-basement lower floor. The sheriff's door was open. Beating his wet hat against his knee, Kyle stepped inside. His face was stiff and wooden, and, to Sheriff Jepson at his desk, it looked dangerous.

"Take a chair," said the sheriff. "Sit down and rest them weary bones."

"Thanks, but no," said Kyle. "I won't be here that long."

Kyle related the scene he had just witnessed, the shooting of Green River.

"Take him to the undertaker," said Kyle. "And charge the burying to me."

"If you want it that way," said the sheriff gently.

"What are you going to do about it?" asked Kyle.

"When you come right down to it," said the sheriff quietly, "I'm afraid the answer is just about nothing."

"*Nothing?*"

"Don't you see?" said the sheriff. "Everything seems to be fixed these days so it comes out nothing."

When Kyle started to speak, the sheriff interrupted him, saying, "Oh, I'll ride out and talk to Mr. Hollister and his friends. In fact I'll go out right now. But you know what they'll say? They'll say they was just trying to do the law a favor, that he was a wanted man. Folks would agree so loud and hard, I doubt if I could scarcely bring them to trial, say nothing of convict them. This is one of the things that happens when manhunt fever takes a place like here today. You know what I seen this morning? I seen the preacher's little seven-year-old boy pertendin' to chase Green River around his front yard with a corncob pistol."

"They didn't give him a chance," said Kyle. "When you want to arrest a man, do you kill him first from the dark?"

"I ain't never did it yet," said the sheriff cheerfully. "But if things keeps on like this, I may have to take it up."

Back in his bedroom, Kyle thought it over. He knew deep in his heart that the sheriff was right. He hadn't done anything, because he couldn't. If you were a really good sheriff, you had at least to obey the law. If you began breaking this rule, doing what people called justice, for instance, pretty soon you thought you were the law yourself. And when you reached that point, what you actually were was an outlaw, and no better, even worse, than the animal you were supposed to curb.

Sometime, someday, Sheriff Jepson was going to decide to act. And that would be a day worth waiting for.

He had had a quick glimpse of the real sheriff with Minnifee, that day out at Delphy's after the burning.

He had just witnessed a cold-blooded execution, and knew it.

Grinnell wanted Green River dead, and made up the robbery thing as an excuse for his gunmen to carry it out without a public fuss.

But why, all at once, did Grinnell want him dead?

It had to be one thing, and one thing only. Those bills of sale. Green River had seen them, and didn't like them, and went to Grinnell and said so. That would be like Green River. And Grinnell had had him wiped out.

But how could all this be? Green River had told Kyle those bills of sale were perfectly legal.

The answer was there somewhere, Kyle knew. But he couldn't find it.

Grinnell, the real Grinnell, was as cold-blooded as Minnifee. And maybe twice as deadly.

Kyle undressed. He was on his bed, almost asleep, when Breathitt popped into his mind.

There was an idea about Breathitt that had been bothering him all along.

A beast like Breathitt, so close to a town, especially a hard-case town like Gaynor, simply could not stay away from it. He could not live like a hermit so near, and yet stay away from its parlor houses and saloons.

117

Now, as he thought about it again, Kyle became convinced that Breathitt must, simply must, have been coming into town secretly to visit its fleshpots. At least occasionally.

This was an angle he had better look into, and soon.

Next morning, about nine, Mr. Flake asked him to go to the freight warehouse to check on a shipment of buggy paint, overdue from St. Louis. The freight warehouse was along the tracks, about three hundred yards south of the depot. It was a long, gray building, barnlike, with a broad loading platform down its front, flush to the track-side. At the north end of the building, an incline, a sloping timber ramp for men and teams, led from the ground up to the platform. Kyle strode up the ramp and had started down the platform when an interesting scene met his eyes.

About thirty feet away was a small knot of people, five to be exact, Mr. Grinnell, Hollister, Wheaton and Baldridge, and the freightmaster. Grinnell was seated in a straight-backed chair before open double doors, and the others were standing in an arc before him, listening to him talk, a polite, almost fawning audience. Sometimes as he spoke, Grinnell would smile faintly, and the others would laugh loudly, sometimes he would frown slightly, and his audience would look angry and sympathetic. He was like an emperor in a moment of relaxation, addressing a few favored subjects. Kyle wondered what subject of conversation could be so fascinating. As he came nearer, he caught words and phrases. Mr. Grinnell was talking about the time,

118

apparently twenty years ago, he had had a boil in his left nostril.

He glanced in Kyle's direction, saw him, and stopped talking. Imperiously, but not hostilely, he raised his finger, crooked its first joint, beckoning, and said, "Fentress, come here."

Kyle was on his way past him anyhow, but he stopped.

A very traditional code was suddenly involved. Only certain people, at certain times, ordered you to 'come here'. A friend could do it, and a boss, of course, and a man who had something to show you, say an elk track. But other people who had something to tell you, even if they were old acquaintances, paid you the respect due by either coming to you, or meeting you half way,

People just didn't talk to each other that way.

The problem was, what should he do?

He had started past him anyway, but he sure didn't want it to look like he was obeying any orders.

He stopped.

Beside his left hand was a small green door with a sign which said, *Private, Freightmaster Only*. He reached out and grasped the china doorknob.

The three gunmen came down the platform toward him. Wheaton said, "You heard the gentleman. He wants to talk to you."

"Then let him yell," said Kyle. "This is as far as I go."

Grinnell, breaking the tension, got up from his chair and joined them, followed by the freightmaster.

Grinnell said, "The business at the hobo camp last night. Where you lost your friend. Lochinvar will pay for the funeral."

"That's been taken care of," said Kyle shortly. "How much did you pay these killers to do it?"

"Nothing. These men work for wages. Like all cowhands."

"Bonus, then? How much bonus after it was did?"

"A hundred dollars apiece."

"You paid them to do it, and you want to pay for the funeral? You really hedge your bets, don't you?"

"I do the right thing as I see it."

The four Lochinvar men walked away down the platform, Grinnell a little in the lead.

The freightmaster cleared his throat. "Leave go of that doorknob. You cain't go into that-there room. Cain't you see it says private? That's my bedroom. What do you want?"

"To ask about a shipment of buggy paint from St. Louis."

Kyle had gotten the buggy-paint order straightened out — it was just plain late — had picked up the mail at the post office, and was approaching the Bluebird Barbershop when the thunderbolt hit him.

The barber was sitting on the bench before his shop window, alone, eating his lunch. He was a short, stocky man with a crest of hair that looked mighty like it had a touch of the curling iron. Beside him on the bench, laid out like tools, was an egg sandwich, two cold biscuits, a dill pickle, a slice of pie, and a cold sweet potato. He peeled the sweet potato, fumbled out a little shaker of salt from his vest pocket, sprinkled it slightly, then a shaker of pepper, repeating the operation, each time with surgical interest, and began to eat.

If there is any man in town that has seen Breathitt, Kyle thought, it's this man. Why didn't I think of it before?

But he'd better be questioned mighty, mighty carefully.

Coming to a halt before him, Kyle said, "That must have been a crackerjack haircut you gave me some time back. I've had a million compliments on it."

"Why, thank you," said the barber, pleased and confused. "I don't recall no other customer bothering to mention it."

"I'm Kyle Fentress," Kyle said.

"I'm E. E. Pangborn. Have a biscuit?"

"I believe not, though they look mighty mouth-waterin'. I'm new in town. I'd like to ask you a question. Where would a feller go to buy a good pocketknife?"

Remembering the display of secondhand cutlery on the barber's shelf inside, Kyle stared him blandly in the face.

"Why right here," said the barber excitedly, getting up. "Not new, but used. And ever'body knows a used knife is better than a new one."

They went inside.

After a bit of pretended haggling, Kyle bought a Barlow with a broken blade, worth no more than a nickle, for twenty cents. He figured this would put the barber in a good mood, and it did.

"A fellow spoke to me the other day in court square," said Kyle. "And I thought by name. I spoke back, to be polite. But for the life of me, I can't remember him."

"The best of us makes mistakes," said the barber, intrigued by this sort of problem. "If he called you by name, you must have knowed him. What did he look like?"

"A big man, in new denims, with a jaw like a hunk of pickled beef."

"That sounds a little like Mr. Whitcomb. Was it by night, or by day?"

"About noon," said Kyle, taking a wild guess.

"Then it couldn't have been Mr. Whitcomb. He doesn't come to town often, and then it's always by night. Generally late at night. You see, since his wife passed away, he's got this big family of children to look after, and he can't get away until they're in bed."

"Is he an old friend of yours? What does he do?"

"No, not an old friend, but a good friend by now. Come to think of it, I don't really know what he does. Except take care of them kids, like I told you."

After a pause, Kyle said, "I guess you met him shaving him, when he come into the shop?"

"I met him shaving him, all right. But he never comes into the shop."

"Don't tell me you go out to his house and do it?"

"No. He comes into my house. I live alone in a little shanty at the edge of town."

"When does he come? Regular?"

"No, not regular. I never know when to expect him. He just shows up at my door at night, with a quart of whisky. I shave him in the kitchen, and then we sit around and drink and visit with each other. You know, get to know each other. My, he's a nice, good-natured man. And when he gets half-soused, he can sing the sweetest romantic ballads. Trouble is, he gets mad if you sing, too."

"Sounds like a wonderful human to know," said Kyle.

He closed his eyes and tried to organize his thoughts. He had made progress here, and yet he had come to a dead end. He couldn't wait all night, every night, at the barber's shanty. It might be weeks before Breathitt reappeared. It might be never.

"That pitch-black hair of his," said Kyle, "looked like it was dyed."

"He ain't got black hair," said the barber. "He's got orange-red hair. You're all mixed up there. Funny thing, though. The first time I seen him. His first visit. He bought a bottle of black hair dye from me. But he never used it. Told me later, he'd changed his mind."

Here was the link, ironclad, between Minnifee and Breathitt. Breathitt had bought the dye, given it to Minnifee, who had used it in the stable, disguising the horse with the white stockings. By now, probably, those stockings were once more white.

"I'll be getting along," said Kyle, moving toward the door. "Hope I don't lose the knife."

"If you do, come back," said the barber happily. "Always glad to be of service."

That afternoon, after lunch, Mr. Flake went to the cupboard under the back stairs, and dragged his big oak medicine chest out into the hall. Like most storekeepers, he could become a rough and ready apothecary if the occasion demanded. As Kyle stood by him, and watched with interest, Mr. Flake fiddled with the colored bottles and jars and cardboard boxes of powders, mixing together a little of this, and a little of that, in an amber-tinted flask. Finally, when he had finished, he handed the flask to Kyle.

"Mrs. Spencer," he said, "has a swelling on her elbow that comes and goes. She must be out of medicine about now. I wonder if you would ride out and give it to her? I would greatly appreciate it."

They stared at each other a hard minute, then cast their eyes aside.

What Mr. Flake meant, of course, was that he was terribly worried about their welfare, and would Kyle go out and check to see if everything was all right?

"Yes, indeed," said Kyle tonelessly. "Glad to."

He reached S-Diamond about suppertime, which Mr. Flake had also doubtless planned, and after he had delivered the medicine, somewhat to Mrs. Spencer's bewilderment, and washed up by the back door, they all sat together around the big table in the dining room. At first, he was a little scared. He had eaten in numerous kitchens, in the saddle, by countless chuckwagons, and once on a stage coach, but, as far as he could remember, this was the first time he had ever eaten in a regular dining room.

"We generally eat in the kitchen," said Barbara, loading his plate with food. "But you're company."

"Not me," said Kyle, pleased yet horrified.

124

The silverware, and the white tablecloth, and the napkins, disturbed him a little at the start, but the food was real ranch food, short ribs cooked with whole onions, mashed potatoes with the short-rib gravy, and hot pumpkin bread with fresh butter and strained honey. Everybody ate plenty, so he ate plenty, too. He wondered once if Barbara and her mother were just eating that way to egg him on, but the idea was foolish and he put it from his mind.

When the meal was finished, he asked them in a careless voice if there had been any more Minnifee trouble, and they said no. He watched their hands when they answered, and their hands were steady, so he believed them.

"My guess is that we've seen the last of him," said Barbara, "that he'll leave us alone from here on out."

But now she twisted her fingers together, and Kyle knew she felt just the opposite.

"Listen," said Kyle. "I'm a cowboy born and bred. That city life is killing me. I want the range so bad I'm almost heartbroke. Why can't I move out here with you folks, and sleep in the barn, say until I get back my health?"

It was Mrs. Spencer who answered. She said, smiling, "I can see you're a physical wreck. Nothing but piano-wire sinews and lean whitleather muscles, and wonder how you even have enough strength to lift that apple tart. But I'm afraid I'm going to have to say no. Barbara's father and I came out here when there was nothing but grass and Indians, and Minnifee and his Turtle Creek Rangers scare me not at all. If they

125

gallivant around me once too often, I'll season them down and make pemmican out of them."

Kyle looked at her in admiration. If there was one thing he revered, it was a good white-hot case of self respect, of personal pride.

"Yes'm," said Kyle, humbly.

"She means it," said Barbara. "And the same goes for me."

But that doesn't make you any safer, thought Kyle.

He said, "About the cow Minnifee killed in your barnyard. Did you report it to the sheriff?"

"No," said Barbara. "It was Lochinvar's cow. We reported it to Mr. Grinnell."

"Did he report it to the sheriff?"

Barbara shook her head. "Mr. Grinnell said the complaint wouldn't equal the baseness of the deed. He'd rather take care of it in some other way."

Kyle said, "Did you think that was a good, decent, law-abiding answer?"

"Yes," said Barbara.

"Well, I don't," said Kyle. "That's what we got courts for." He pushed back his chair and got up. "Thank you for the wonderful meal. I'll never forget it. I'd better be on my way. I'll have to push my mare a little at that. I want to be back around nine-thirty."

He pushed Effie on the return to Gaynor. He enjoyed it, and she enjoyed it. He was back in town, in the Star Stable, by nine-fifteen.

He had things to do at the store before he went to bed, and plenty of them, though Mr. Flake hadn't so much as suggested them.

Tomorrow was court-day.

For days now, when people weren't talking about Minnifee and Grinnell, about Green River or the three Lochinvar gunmen, they had been talking about it.

Deep within him, Kyle too was keyed up. It was something to get keyed up over.

CHAPTER
TWELVE

Court-day morning was crystal clear, with crisp, tangy autumn air and amethyst and rose sunlight. Kyle had seen many a court-day before, and knew it to be important to the town not only from a festive viewpoint, but from a mercantile viewpoint, too. On this day, the sitting of the court, the Red Front should do a big business.

Outlying folk, ranchers, farmers, homesteaders, would come to town to shop, to meet old friends rarely seen, to transact little business deals. By mid-morning, Gaynor's streets and back streets were choked with buggies and buck-boards and wagons, its corrals jammed with mustangs and riding mules. At the hitching racks on Main Street you could see anything from homemade wooden stirrups to worked leather saddles with solid-silver conchos. Men gathered in doorways of shops to chew and talk, women, wooden-faced to be mannerly, paraded the boardwalk, and little children yelled, and looped, and scooted everywhere. Merchandise, most of it — but not Mr. Flake's — marked up for the day, went like hotcakes.

Twice Mr. Flake, with an understanding glint in his eye, asked Kyle if he would like to go to the square —

the center of activity — and look around. But Kyle, because of the bustle and rush of customers in the store, seeing how badly he was needed, said no.

A little after noon, when the country folk, who were used to eating sharply by the clock, were having box lunches on wagon seats and on lawns of householders, and when there was a lull in the Red Front, he did go.

Court square was crowded and seemed to be taking no lunch. This was the day of hagglers, traders, swappers. And in little knots and gatherings, they were busy at it. These free-lance businessmen fell into two classes. Amateurs, farmers and ranchers, with gunlocks, ploy points, and countless other odds and ends for sale or swap, with their wives nearby, with mounds of pumpkins, baskets of lush grapes, jugs of sorghum, eager for barter, and professionals. The professionals were mainly horse traders, grimey, villainous-looking men with eyes like molten glass, displaying a single horse, perhaps, or a string of horses.

A fat man in a canvas lean-to shelter was selling bowls of bean soup loaded with red peppers and big hunks of sow belly, with a side dish of pones, and Kyle, suddenly crazy with hunger, stopped and ate.

A man came up by his elbow and also ate. He ate with long, relishing slurps. It was Sheriff Jepson. The sheriff neither looked at him, nor spoke to him. And Kyle, who had antennae a mile long when it came to being rebuffed, ignored the sheriff too. And did a pointed job of it. Today, in his holster, the sheriff wore a different gun, one that Kyle had never seen. An old relic, with a greasy walnut grip, the steel bluing worn off in patches from the cylinder and gone entirely from the spur of the hammer.

When he had finished, the sheriff said to the counterman, "Have you got a toothpick, friend?"

"A toothpick for bean soup?" said the counterman. "That's a new one on me."

"Then just say no," said the sheriff gently. "Next court-day I'll bring my own."

The sheriff put down the empty bowl, turned around, and faced the crowd.

He'd had it timed like clockwork, Kyle later realized.

Off a little distance to the left was a farm wagon, loaded with winter squash and turnips and cabbage, with its tail gate down. Mr. Grinnell stood by a rear wheel, laughing and joking with the owner. As the sheriff turned, Grinnell waved good-bye to the farmer and headed toward the bean-soup stand. There was a clearing in the crowd a few feet before the stand, and Grinnell seemed casually directing his steps toward it.

At the same time, not far to the right, Minnifee's head, slightly above other heads, could be seen nodding and speaking to friends as he pushed his tall, lithe body through the assembly. He, also, was headed directly toward the little open space before Kyle and the sheriff.

"Let's hope they take it out in words," said Sheriff Jepson, finally addressing Kyle. "Words don't maim innocent women and children." He slipped his gun in its leather, and hung his fingers on his belt buckle.

Minnifee and Grinnell came out into the little clearing, met full face, and stopped about five feet apart.

Grinnell seemed to enjoy it. Minnifee, on the other hand, seemed to Kyle slightly nervous about it. His face was domineering, arrogant, but his frame was unnaturally stiff. This wouldn't be the way he would want it, Kyle knew. Not equal, and public, face to face without trickery.

The crowd drew hastily back, enlarging the perimeter.

Deliberately, dispassionately, Grinnell abused Minnifee with words. Not obscene words, or profanity, but with icy contemptuous words which left him with no manhood whatever, which almost stripped the flesh from his body. Minnifee took them at first, then went ashen and spastic around the mouth.

"What did you do before you ranched?" said Grinnell derisively. "Slop pigs?"

"I've always ranched," said Minnifee. "My father had one of the largest outfits in Texas." Drawing himself together, cutting his eyes this way and that, taking in the hypnotized crowd, he said loudly, "We don't need people like you here. Spending eastern money to kill nice old men like Mr. Delphy."

Grinnell slapped him. He slapped him left-handedly across the cheek, and Minnifee's jaw went askew beneath the force of the blow. Like they used to say of mules, Kyle thought, jipjawed. Minnifee went back a half step, his spurs caught and tangled, his ankles crossed, and he sprawled to one knee, his stiff canvas coat ballooning up over his ear. Wildly, he fought his thigh-gun half out of its holster. And Grinnell shot him with an overlapping fusillade.

Kyle studied the crowd. It was forcing itself to call it a fair fight. Grinnell had shot him at a mean disadvantage, but what else could he have done? Their faces said Grinnell had no other choice, but yet, somehow, it seemed a shame.

To Kyle, it seemed more than a shame. It seemed a sort of lesson. Here was a man, he thought, who went around top-heavy with guns, two of them, who never got around to using any of them.

Kyle stepped forward and bent over Minnifee. He was dead all right, but under the gaze of the crowd, breaking and advancing, he put his ears to Minnifee's lips, and looked intent, pretending to listen.

The sheriff's hand touched Kyle's shoulder, moving him aside. By the sheriff was Gaynor's doctor.

"One hundred and two percent dead-o," announced the doctor briskly, after his examination.

The sheriff took Kyle a little to one side. "Did he say anything to you before he passed on?"

"Yes," said Kyle.

"What?"

"He said he was sorry he'd spent such a low-down, trouble-making life."

The sheriff stared at him skeptically.

After a moment, thinking of other things, the sheriff said, "Why don't you drop into my office, say in a half hour?"

Kyle nodded. He wondered why, but asked no questions.

Minnifee was taken away, and the crowd dispersed. Almost before Kyle could roll a brown paper cigarette, men were buying horses again, women were selling vegetables, and little children were hammering across

132

the dry earth, calling and laughing. The sheriff had gone, and he was standing alone, when Mr. E. E. Pangborn, the barber at the Bluebird, came up to him. He could hardly contain himself from curiosity. "What did he say to you?"

"What did who say to who?"

"Minnifee to you. Just before he died. We all saw it."

"I don't know if I should pass it on."

"I'm a barber. We're like doctors and lawyers. We can keep our mouths shut."

"It was something about somebody no one seems interested in any more. It was about Mr. Spencer."

"What about Mr. Spencer, poor Mr. Spencer?"

After a long hesitation, Kyle said, "He told me who killed him."

Pangborn's eyes stuck out like hard-boiled eggs. "Think of that. Who?"

"I ain't sure just now, just at the moment, whether or not I want to make it public."

"Why not?" said Pangborn, eagerly.

"He might not have knowed what he was saying. He was mighty bad hurt, just on the edge of death, give or take a little. He might have even been unconscious."

"Oh, he was conscious all right," said Pangborn. "We all seen the gleam in his eye when he leaned forward and whispered in your ear."

"I don't know," said Kyle. "I'd better think it over."

He watched the excited, but disappointed man walk away. All day long he'd be telling it to customers. Maybe tonight, he'd be telling it to Breathitt himself.

A stranger coming into the sheriff's office with Kyle, Kyle decided, might well think Grinnell, sitting behind the sheriff's desk, head tilted back, at ease, with one of his crooked cigars in his mouth, was the sheriff: and that the sheriff himself, standing modestly before the desk, wilted and weary-looking, was, say, a back-country stockman reporting a lost hound dog. As Kyle entered, the sheriff said, "Take a chair, Mr. Fentress. I'll be with you in a minute." Kyle sat down on a chair against the wall.

Grinnell said curtly, "Well, I'm here. You asked me to come and I came. What do you want? Are you going to arrest me for the little incident just now in court square? It was self-defense. You were there. You saw it. You and a hundred others."

"No," said the sheriff. "I ain't going to arrest you. Whether I'd like to or not is something else again."

"Then what did you want?" Grinnell looked annoyed. "I'm a busy man."

"I wanted to tell you to tighten up your rein a little."

"Just a friendly warning, eh?"

"Not especially friendly," said the sheriff mildly.

Grinnell got angrily to his feet. "You could be talking the wrong way to the wrong man, you know. You'll be up again for office again sometime. And Lowden, Lokely, and Lamont can have a lot to do with elections."

From his chair, Kyle said, "Mr. Jepson?"

The sheriff turned to him. "Yes, son?"

"You aiming to run for sheriff of Boston?"

134

"No, son, I ain't," said the sheriff kindly. "Mr. Grinnell is mixed up."

Grinnell's cheeks turned a deep, savage purple.

"And there's another matter I'd like to explain to you," said the sheriff, with just the tiniest touch of hidden chill to his voice. "The range war is over. Mr. Minnifee is dead. They ain't nobody, no group, no organization, again Lochinvar now. You don't need Mr. Wheaton, Mr. Baldridge, and Mr. Hollister no longer. They're finished hereabouts."

"And now you're trying to tell me," said Grinnell, "who I can hire and who I can't. For your information, they might very well become permanent out at Three L."

"You see," said Kyle conversationally. "When a man hires gunmen, it gets into his blood. He thinks he's bigger than he was before."

"You mean," said the sheriff, appearing to try to understand, "that he's really littler?"

"Not exactly that," said Kyle. "Because he has to be mighty little to start with, to do it."

"It's really an interesting subject, ain't it?" said the sheriff. He seemed naively fascinated at Kyle's statement.

"It sure is," said Kyle. "I've seen strange things come out of it in my day. I mind a thing that happened once when I was working up in Montana. A rancher hired a couple of gunmen to get him out of a little difficulty. Time passed, and the trouble passed too, but the feller kept them on. People didn't like it, but they were afraid of these gunmen, and at first they didn't know what to do."

"What did they do?" asked the sheriff.

"They did the sensible thing, they killed the feller that hired them, because he was only a tolerable shot. I understand they laid about seven ambushes that missed. But the eighth got him. Someone blowed off the lower half of his face with a muzzle-loading shotgun filled with birdshot and horseshoe nails."

Bleakly, Grinnell said, "You don't scare me a bit." They knew this was the truth. He left the room.

When he had gone, the sheriff said, "Next stop, I guess, is the Elkhorn."

When the three Lochinvar gunmen were in tow, this was their favorite hangout. Everybody knew it. Some people stayed away from it, some came to bask in their presence. Kyle stayed strictly away; he didn't want to bring on any unnecessary difficulty.

Now he said, "Okay. Let's go."

"Not us, me," said the sheriff. "You ain't invited." When Kyle started to speak, he said gravely, "And don't mess with me, son."

When he had gone, Kyle left too, fast. He loped through the crowd in the square, entered the Red Front by the alley, hitched on his gunbelt, and was waiting by the door of the Elkhorn Cafe when Sheriff Jepson wandered up.

"Scat," said the sheriff, from the corner of his mouth. He stepped inside; Kyle followed.

Kyle, in his day, had been inside some pretty mean saloons, but the Elkhorn Cafe, he sensed instantly,

136

came pretty close to being among the lowest. For one thing, he recognized the sorry kind of bartender behind the bar and had the feeling that the bartender, immediately, placed him for the kind of gun-kid he had been in the past. These things, building up from tough experience, became almost intuitive.

The window and the door pane had been painted black, and the room was lighted by an old camphene lamp hanging from an S-hook, a rusty-iron slaughtering hook, from a rafter overhead. There was a short bar, with a crude home-made backbar behind it, and six or seven miscellaneous tables with chairs. The floor was covered with shredded tanbark. There were a couple of shabby barflies at the bar, and back in the rear of the room, at a table, sat Baldridge, Wheaton, and Hollister. There was a half-empty quart whiskey bottle on the center of the table, and the tabletop was covered with empty beer bottles. Boilermakers. They had probably been at that table since they arrived in town, and wouldn't leave until midnight. This was their court-day. At first, when the sheriff and Kyle approached and stood by the table, they showed no expression whatever.

Expressionless and silent, but their silence was not drunken, it was arrogant.

Finally, Wheaton said, "It's the sheriff and that kid again." To them, he said, "Move on. This cafe's full."

Speaking quietly, the sheriff said, "I hope you men haven't run up too big a bill here."

Half-amused, Baldridge said, "Why?"

"Because I'm going to pay it," said the sheriff.

They stared at him.

"Pay it?" said Wheaton. "Why?"

"Because you're fixing to leave this place, and this town, and this county, so fast you won't have time."

Baldridge and Hollister laughed. Wheaton said, "We work for Lochinvar. We don't take orders from nobody but Mr. Grinnell."

"Get to your feet, and move," said the sheriff.

There was a moment of stillness, of malignant intensity.

At last, Hollister said, "It's hard to kill a sheriff and get away with it. But it can be did."

"What you got in mind?" said Wheaton.

Frowning, Hollister said, "Nobody is going to run me out of nowhere. Such a thing ain't good for your reputations, and in our trade reputations is what means money. We'll say the kid drawed on us, and we defended ourselves, and the sheriff and the kid got killed in the cross fire."

The other two nodded, their mouths wet, cat-hungry.

"It may work," said Kyle critically. As though he had been asked for his advice. "On the other hand, it may not. We'll just have to try it and see."

Now it was he, Kyle, who was the focus of their eyes. They seemed to be really seeing him for the first time.

"You stay out of this, you smart aleck," said the sheriff angrily.

From behind the bar, the bartender said, "Somehow, he don't look like no smart aleck to me."

"Don't be stupid, Sheriff," said Wheaton, suddenly reasonable. "Hain't you got no idee, no idee at all, what you're up against? Gunfighting ain't a matter of high hopes, it's a matter of skill, split-second skill. Why don't you walk out of here and forget the whole thing? You don't stand a chance."

The sheriff took a little square of paper from his vest pocket and laid it on the tabletop. One by one, they picked it up, read it, and passed it on. Hollister and Baldridge read it with difficulty, moving their lips. When they returned it to the table, Kyle, in turn reached for it. It was an old receipt from the local cemetery for one lot, made out to Sheriff Clyde L. Jepson.

"I may as well use it right now as anytime," said the sheriff.

He spoke so casually, and so sincerely, that a chill went up the nape of Kyle's neck.

The gunmen arose. Wheaton said, "We're leaving. But not because you are ordering us to. We're just moving on. To us, you and this town are nothing."

"That ain't good enough," said the sheriff.

"What do you mean?" asked Baldridge.

"You're leaving because I'm ordering you to. You ain't leaving because I'm inviting you to, or suggesting or advising you to. Or because you were just somehow fixin' to go anyhow. You're leaving because the sheriff of this county has kicked you out, officially. I just don't want no misunderstanding on this point."

"Have it your way," said Wheaton hastily.

Now, they seemed anxious to go.

After they had gone, the bartender spoke to Kyle. He spoke to him in deference, though he had never seen him before. He asked, "Were they good? I'd like your opinion. Were they really good?"

Being addresssed that way, in this kind of a place, by this kind of a man, the years slipped back on Kyle, and he was living for the briefest instant in the past. Honestly, scarcely realizing what he said, he answered, "You never know, of course. But in my judgement, I've seen better, and I've seen worse."

Out on the sidewalk with the sheriff, Kyle said, "A while back, when we were in your office with Mr. Grinnell, the thing I've been looking for finally hit me."

"What?" said the sheriff.

"Will you do me a favor? Go out to the Lochinvar with me tomorrow? We'll take Mr. Flake."

"Why?" said the sheriff. "And why Mr. Flake?"

"You'll see."

Business at the Red Front stayed active the rest of the day, into early evening when the wagons and riding mules, and buggies and buckboards, began to parade out of town. The hunch in his mind that the fake story he had given Pangborn, the barber, would bring Breathitt out of his hole, to him, grew increasingly emphatic. He kept a sharp eye open, on everyone.

As soon as Breathitt heard it, and he would certainly hear it, he would believe that Kyle, of all living persons, could connect him with Mr. Spencer's killing.

Being the stupid savage animal he was, he would think the only thing to do would be shut Kyle's mouth, and quick.

If desperation overcame him, and he struck in daylight somewhere, and Kyle was unarmed, it would be too bad. But this was highly improbable. Being the man he was, he'd likely strike at night, stealthily. He didn't come that night.

CHAPTER
THIRTEEN

They left Gaynor early for Lochinvar — the sheriff, Kyle and Mr. Flake. Mr. Flake, in his townsman's broadcloth, proved, somewhat to Kyle's surprise, to be as good and as natural a horseman as any of them. He was a sick man, though, and showed it. But it was important he come along. He could very well be the factor that settled the whole thing.

"I'm going into this blind," said the sheriff. "Because I trust you."

"So am I," said Mr. Flake. "And for the same reason. In the past, I've found it paid."

"I could be wrong," said Kyle, suddenly showing pressure.

He gave them a look, and said, "Let's go by S-Diamond."

Puzzled, neither of the men said anything. Finally, the sheriff said, "Why not? It's on our way."

Barbara and her mother were mixing a barrel of brine for pickling their winter's pork when their guests arrived. They were welcomed, seated in the parlor, and given coffee and beefsteak sandwiches. Mr. Flake hung his hat on his knee. The sheriff, abruptly realizing he had not yet uncovered, placed his hat carefully on the floor, by his boot. Kyle followed the sheriff's suit, for this was the mannerly custom he was acquainted with.

After a little general comment on the weather, and the coming of winter, Kyle edged into the conversation, and turned it blandly to the subject of Lochinvar.

"How many Three L cows does S-Diamond graze?" he asked.

"My," said Mrs. Spencer. "A good many."

"How many?"

"That's pretty hard to say," said Barbara. "Why? Is there some special reason behind your question?"

The sheriff, interested all at once, said, "You mean you just graze them, and don't know how many?"

"Grazing, as you know," said Barbara, "is rented off two different ways. Sometimes there's a rough toll-price per cow, very general and very rough, say so much per hundred. That's so the renter doesn't deluge your land with stock, and grub it clean out. Or sometimes, when you can trust the renter, you just rent the land and leave it up to him. That's the way we do with Mr. Grinnell."

"And he's honest with you?" asked the sheriff.

"Yes, indeed," said Mrs. Spencer. "He never overloads us. I've been looking at cows all my life, and I'd know. He just puts in the right number of cows for the grass."

"Then why can't you figure how many he grazes here?" asked Kyle. "You see them all the time. Why can't you estimate them?"

"He's got his own personal theory on grazing," said Barbara. "He's explained it to us many times. He

143

moves them from pasture to pasture, from range to range, in and out — at least twice as often as another rancher would. Most ranchers think too much moving takes meat off of them. But Mr. Grinnell says new range gives them new appetite, and this more than makes up for it."

"Last time I heard a speech like that," said Kyle, "I heard it from a man in an alley in Denver. He had a little table, and three shells, and a pea."

They didn't much care for his comment.

He said, "The things that man could do with that pea! You kept thinking it was one place, and it wasn't there at all. In fact it wasn't anywhere, but under his fingernail, or in his palm."

The sheriff looked thoughtful, but confused. Mr. Flake said, "What are you getting at?"

Kyle asked, "What kind of a neighbor is Mr. Grinnell?"

"You couldn't ask for better," said Barbara.

"He was a fine neighbor, and a fine renter," said Mrs. Spencer judiciously, "until Mr. Minnifee got on his high horse, you might say. And now that Mr. Minnifee has passed on to his reward —"

"Very well put," said Mr. Flake.

"And now that Mr. Minnifee is gone, Mr. Grinnell will get rid of his three gunmen and go back to old times."

"I heard someplace," said the sheriff, "that them three fellers have already gone."

"Well, that's good news," said Mrs. Spencer. "I must confess I never really liked them."

To Kyle, Barbara said, "You just happened to come into the county at the wrong time. Until Mr. Minnifee began to cause trouble, Lochinvar was bubbling with prosperity and good fellowship. Big Fourth of July and Christmas parties for the hands, higher pay than any other ranch in the county, friendly and hospitable and polite to the whole countryside."

"My," said the sheriff, getting to his feet. "You make it sound like a paradise."

"Come to think of it," said Barbara, "that's just about what it was."

Standing in the middle of the parlor rug the gentlemen, considering themselves to have adequately carried out high-fashion etiquette, fitted on their hats. They all felt better immediately.

"Take good care of yourself, Hannah," Mr. Flake said fondly to Mrs. Spencer.

They left.

When they rode into the Lochinvar ranchyard, Mr. Grinnell was leaning on his office doorway. The muscles of his face became completely still as they came up, and his eyes, behind the lenses of his spectacles, erased themselves of any emotion or message whatever. They dismounted without speaking, tied up their horses to the rail, and stepped past him, inside. He followed them in and closed the door.

There was nothing friendly or social about this visit, and no one, including Grinnell himself, made any pretense that there might be.

Grinnell seated himself behind his desk. He tried to do it in his old emperor-and-rabble style, but there was something missing. Not much, just that true bred-in-the-bone insolence always there before. Working hard at it, he came up with a pretty good imitation, but not good enough.

It was hard to believe, but Kyle was convinced that the very sight of them, and of the sheriff with his star, maybe, turned Mr. Grinnell sick with fright.

Smart as he was, with no specific reason, he was away ahead of them. He knew that this was it.

Knew that this was it, but was a bulldog for hanging on.

They would have to beat him down, Kyle decided. And that wasn't going to be easy. And there better not be any mistakes.

All Kyle's wonderful new world, the Flakes, the sheriff, Barbara, everything, hung in the balance. Hung on the way Kyle handled it.

Then, almost immediately, to Kyle's surprise, Grinnell took the offensive.

He said severely, "I heard what happened at the Elkhorn yesterday, Sheriff. In spite of my warning to you on the subject. I am writing my superiors in Boston and informing them how you are interfering with our functioning here. I'm afraid you are about to learn what it is like to be up against real power, power you can't even comprehend."

"You better telegraph them," said Kyle. "Because that's what we're going to do."

"You're going to telegraph who?" said Grinnell. "I don't quite understand."

"Those bosses of yours you're talking about," said Kyle. "Lowden, Lokely, and Lamont, up in Boston."

"I hardly think they'll pay much attention to your telegram," said Grinnell, disdainfully. "I'm their manager."

"Right now," said Kyle. "But what about this time tomorrow?"

"What do you mean?"

"Our telegram to them is going to say, 'Your manager at Lochinvar is swindling you. Better investigate.'"

Without batting an eye, Grinnell said, "Any big corporation is accustomed to receiving wild and groundless communications. They've got a special big wastebasket for them. I wouldn't advise it. It wouldn't help your case."

He was so calm about it, he almost sidetracked Kyle.

"Is he really doing it?" said the sheriff. "Cheating his owners?"

"Cheating isn't the word," said Kyle. "It's bigger'n than that. Plunderin' is a better word."

"But how could he?" said Mr. Flake. "Running a ranch is a very uncomplicated business and its records are simple and obvious. The slightest defalcation or irregularity would become immediately apparent."

"He pads his buying lists," said Kyle. "Say he goes down in Texas and buys cows, and gets genuine bills of sale. All right. Then when he gets back, he enters in his records that he bought more cows than he really did. The extra money, the difference on these ghost cows, he turns back to himself."

"But every year," said Mr. Flake, "when his books are audited, if they are audited, there would be this discrepancy. And if they weren't audited this thing would pile up and accumulate and grow until it was ridiculous."

"I'm afraid Mr. Fentress is no accountant," said Grinnell, but his face was white around the jowls.

"I imagine his books are shipshape," said Kyle. "He probably balances them every year, and to the penny. But here's the way he must do it. He puts these missing cows down to natural range loss, to natural hazards. If you'd look through his records, you'd find Lochinvar's range loss is mighty high, but how can Boston tell?"

"It so happens," said Grinnell, "that our annual losses are high, but whose aren't these days, with blizzards, and wolves, and rustlers, and so forth?"

"You've just listened to a letter from Lochinvar's manager to the home office," said Kyle.

"Think of that," said the sheriff. He seemed to be enjoying the conversation immensely.

I better be right, thought Kyle. But I am. I have to be.

"That's why he shuttles his cows here and there, over the range," said Kyle. "Making their number hard to estimate. That's why Mrs. Spencer says she sees a good many, but doesn't know how many."

"My books are open to inspection any time anyone wants to look at them," said Grinnell.

"So is a pair of loaded dice," said Kyle. "So everything is going along all right, and then we got

Minnifee and real trouble in the county, and then Hollister, Wheaton, and Baldridge."

"I don't quite foller you," said the sheriff. "Not just there."

"Who does?" said Grinnell.

"I do," said Mr. Flake.

Kyle had the feeling he was just throwing in his support.

"When Minnifee got this cravin' for being important, and picked Lochinvar to jump on, and started his crazy rumor, a complete lie, about Three L cows being stolen, he put Mr. Grinnell in danger. The cows, themselves, were as honest as the day was long, what there was of them, and I'm sure Minnifee really believed it, but Mr. Grinnell got wild at the idea he was under any kind of suspicion at all. So he brought in Hollister, Wheaton, and Baldridge to stop Minnifee."

"I brought them in to stop a range war," said Grinnell. "And they did."

"Well," said the sheriff. "I guess that's one way of looking at it. To stop the range war."

"One day it come to me," said Kyle, "that if somebody could get a look at the Lochinvar bills of sale, and prove definite that the cattle weren't stolen, that would save the county a lot of bloodshed. Green River said he could pick a safe and went in with me on the idea and got into the Lochinvar safe."

When no one spoke, Kyle said, "He saw the bills of sale. They were honest, he said, but they bothered him."

"Why?" said the sheriff.

"This part's a guess," said Kyle. "If you and Mr. Flake want to walk out on me, this, sure in hell, is the time to do it."

"I'm happy where I am," said the sheriff. "Go on."

"He looked at the bills of sale, and then, to be absolutely careful, he must have cross-checked them in the company's books. He seen the books showed more cows than the range did. And he knew about the range, for he was tallyman and had made out the tally sheets. Green River was an honest man from the pinch in his hat down to his boot soles. He went to Grinnell, and asked him to explain it."

"And?" said the sheriff.

"And Grinnell made up the robbery story, and set his gunmen on Green River to wipe him out. Which they did."

Grinnell tried to speak, failed, and simply shook his head.

Kyle said, "And they would have wiped me out, too, if I'd acted like Green River had told me anything. I was really walking on ice them days."

Grinnell said, "But still no proof."

"We're fixing to get the proof," Kyle said. "That's why we brought along Mr. Flake, to give us a little hand. He's a merchant and a bookkeeper. He wants to compare Green River's tally sheets with your recorded, and bogus, purchase records."

"That's all," said the sheriff.

There was a long interval of silence.

Finally, Grinnell crumpled.

150

"It's banked in St. Louis," he said brokenly. "I'll restore every penny. Tell Lowden, Lokely, and Lamont I'll restore it."

"Who is going to restore Green River?" asked Kyle.

Gaynor was mostly dark, the Red Front showed a feeble night light and Melinda had gone to bed, when Kyle and Mr. Flake returned. The sheriff had lodged his prisoner in a cell, for the moment charged with conspiracy of murder. Mr. Flake, exhausted, said goodnight to Kyle at the stairwell in the back hall, and in turn retired.

Kyle lit the lamp in the kitchen and drank a tepid cup of coffee. He took the lighted lamp into his bedroom and placed it on his washstand. He crossed the hall to the storeroom, opened the door about two inches, and set his gun belt, heavy with leather and cartridges, just the way he liked it. Through the partly-open storeroom door, he could see a slice of the dark hall, his closed bedroom door, and the lamplight from its keyhole and threshold. He waited.

He wondered how many nights he would wait this way. Many men were tortured. Kyle neither liked it, or disliked it. When he had to do it, it was a job, and he treated it like any other job. Conscientiously and patiently.

It must have been about three-thirty when Breathitt came.

He came Indian-quiet; nevertheless Kyle heard him. He heard him flip the lock in the mortise lock on the alley door with his skeleton key. (You could buy one at any hardware store.) He heard the muted and almost inaudible creaking, as he came forward along the passage. Then the light from the keyhole disappeared and the light at the threshold became blotted with two boots.

For an instant, the figure stood motionless. Then, softly, Breathitt opened the door and the light fell full upon him.

His gun was in his hand, and his face, clean-shaven — fresh from Pangborn's razor certainly — was ugly and meaty and venomous. His denims were not so new anymore; he had been sleeping in them on the bare ground, probably, and they were rumpled and clay-smeared.

Kyle said, "All right. Don't move. Don't even hardly breathe."

Breathitt seemed to turn into a statue. In a way, you might say this was a skill, too. Freezing on order. A life-saving technique, where a mistake could be fatal.

"Put your gun in its holster," said Kyle.

Breathitt, who had expected it to be taken from him, complied warily.

"And now that you got that door already open," said Kyle. "Step in."

Breathitt obeyed. Kyle followed him inside the bedroom.

"What you going to do?" said Breathitt.

"That's hard to say," said Kyle. "We'll have to wait and see. You killed Mr. Spencer, didn't you?"

"I understand that's what Minnifee told you when he died."

"He told me nothing. He was dead."

Breathitt grinned. "Well, think of that."

"But it wouldn't really have made no difference anyhow," said Kyle. "If I'd have claimed so in a court of law, you could have said no, and walked out a free man. They don't hang a man without proof."

Breathitt became suddenly relaxed. "I never thought of it that way. Stop aiming that gun at me, and I'll answer your question."

Kyle holstered his weapon.

"Yes, I done it," said Breathitt. "But it took two tries."

"On Minnifee's orders?"

"Right."

"What did Minnifee have against Mr. Spencer?"

"Nothing."

"Against Grinnell, then?"

"Nothing."

When Kyle's face showed no response, Breathitt said thickly, "They was a lot to Mr. Minnifee that didn't meet the eye. I've worked for a lot of bosses in my day, but he was the smartest."

"Until he got his spurs tangled up," said Kyle.

"He was nobody, you see, and he had this idea that if you stirred up enough trouble you was bound to profit some way. Like he kept saying to me, if the other fellow loses, you gotta win. That's a law of nature."

"Life is like a big faro game?"

"Sure."

"You were the one that burned out Delphy. Or helped."

"Me, and Minnifee and Delphy himself. The idea was to stir up Grinnell. And it worked."

"It sure did. It got Delphy dead, too."

Gradually, Breathitt was becoming a new man. The savage, self-assured beast that Kyle had met under the railroad trestle.

"When Hollister and his two pals came into the picture," said Kyle. "Did they worry you?"

"No," said Breathitt, and Kyle believed him. "It's fellows like that that makes good business."

"One more question," said Kyle. "When you killed Mr. Spencer, why didn't you wipe out Miss Barbara and her mother, too?"

"I wasn't asked to."

"You would if you'd been asked?"

"Why not? It's a trade."

"Ever killed a woman yet?"

"Not up to now. They ain't much scalp money on women."

Kyle said, "Breathitt, why do you think I give you back your gun?"

Breathitt tightened.

"Not to carry out that door," said Kyle.

Breathitt made a pretty good draw, but Kyle had a feeling that maybe Wheaton, with his little .38, could have nosed him out.

Kyle shot him.

Kyle's hand lifted, almost limply, and his gun was out of its holster, and he shot Breathitt twice in the heart. Once for Mrs. Spencer, and once for Barbara. It was the draw, so simple-looking, so seemingly relaxed, and yet so accurate, that, in the past, for about a year and a half had made him famous in certain circles throughout three states. The weapon was hardly seen before it was heard and then there it was, afterwards, big and clumsy-looking in his careless fist.

After it had happened, he was ashamed of himself.

Here am I, always preaching about courts of law, he thought — and now this.

From the hall upstairs, he heard quick, sleepy footsteps.

He stopped Mr. Flake at the bedroom doorway.

"Go get the sheriff," he said, "while I keep Melinda out."

Just before dawn came a lashing rain. By breakfast time, it had turned to bruising, granulated snow. Sheepskins and felt boots appeared on Main Street. By supper, the temperature had plunged far below zero. Kyle, behind his counter, thought of what the out-country would be like in the morning, of desperate ranchers combing the range, assessing damage. He thought of the days to come, of shell-like bunk-houses in the evening with their inadequate cherry-red cannonball stoves. And of the incoming riders, blue with cold, their sheepskins glazed with ice.

Barbara, hearing of Grinnell's arrest, had come into town to learn the details. That night, after the store was closed, they sat in the kitchen — Melinda, Barbara, and Mr. Flake — discussing it.

When the conversation had worn itself out, Mr. Flake produced mugs of hot mulled cider, flavored with cinnamon and each floating a single fragrant clove.

The buckshot ice of the blizzard scratched frantically against the kitchen window.

"There was an old Cheyenne in the store about a week ago," said Mr. Flake. "He claimed it was going to be a mighty hard winter."

"Cold," said Kyle, "and I mean *real* cold, can be bad."

He rested the warm mug pleasantly on his knee.

THE END